This is about Henry please read it.

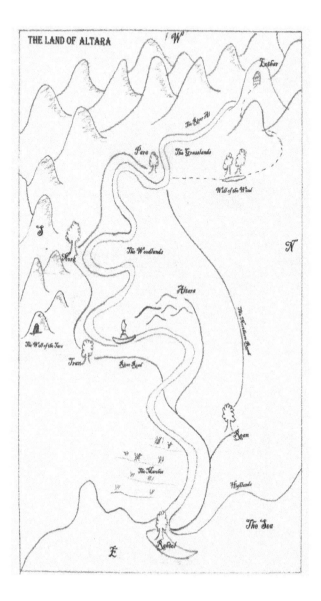

THE LAND OF ALTARA

A Suborediom Novel

HENRY ON FIRE

By Stuart

Bradley Stuart Books
U. S. A.

To Pam who has always believed in me and who has helped me find my fire.

Henry on Fire
By Stuart
Copyright ©2012 Stuart E. Schadt
All rights reserved. Published by Bradley Stuart Books.

Printed in the United States of America.

ISBN 978-0-6156-7565-7

First Edition

Related short stories can be found at:
www.henryonfire.com

Contents

Chapter 1 Sunday Night

Elvis left the building, Dorothy left Kansas and last night I left the neighborhood. I am trying to wrap my head around what happened. I got this idea to write my story in a journal. Maybe I'm only doing this for me I don't know. (But I want to think someone else cares enough to be reading this. I hope you care enough to stick with me. Thanks for reading.)

I went to bed about ten as usual. The weekend had been okay, definitely nothing to write about. My life is pretty ordinary. I suffocate in the quiet boredom of suburbia. I live outside D.C., in Fairdale. I tell people I live in Suborediom, Virginia. They usually give me a weird look. Sometimes they even say, 'Where's that?' (You get it, don't you? Suburbia + Boredom = Suborediom. I really want you to understand.)

I woke up at 1 a.m., wide wake. I couldn't figure out what woke me. I had been dreaming, something about a horse and pain but I couldn't quite remember. My eyes searched my room as my ears searched the house. I heard Mom and Dad snoring, two rooms away. No sound came from Larry's room. (He's my little brother.)

I rolled over, to go back to sleep, but the moonlight drew my attention outside. A horse stood in my front yard, a real horse! His coat shone silver in the moonlight. His face had a white mark, a star, between his eyes. He stared right at me. Our eyes locked for a minute or two.

After our staring contest, I decided to head outside. I wanted to touch this horse. I've talked about slipping out at night before, but I never have. Fred and Jamal say they would meet me, but I doubt they would show. (They're my only friends.)

I slipped silently down the hall toward the front door. The first lock made a loud, snapping noise. I froze and listened. I heard nothing different. I flipped the second one more gently. I opened the door and checked the locks to make sure I wouldn't be locked out. The horse was standing twenty feet away from me. As I crossed the lawn, I felt my heart pounding in my chest.

I approached carefully. I learned what little I know about horses on a one hour ride in a national park. Our horses followed the ranger's horse for an hour. The white spot on his forehead is called a star and you approach a horse slowly with your hand held out, open and palm up. That's everything I remember. I hope somebody taught this horse the same rules. He shook his head and snorted. I jumped back and wiped horse snot off my face. I approached again. I started to sweat and my legs were weak, but I wanted to touch the horse.

The white mark on his forehead was more a scar, than a star. I laid my hand on his neck for a minute. He pulled away. He circled around the front yard and came back. A connection was building between me and this horse. This is the horse from my dream. He wanted something from me, and I needed to figure out what it was. Again I laid my hand on his neck and again he pulled away, but this time he trotted down the street a few houses. My heart sank at first, but then I knew he wanted me to come with him. As soon as I understood what he wanted he turned around and came back. With no saddle and no reins and for about a dozen other reasons I can think of, leaving on this horse would be a bad idea.

Even though he turned around to come back, I had decided to call it quits. I had my hand on the door when he came and stood beside the porch. The fact he knew enough to stand by the porch so I could climb on his back overcame my fear and my sense of reason. I scrambled over the porch rail and slid my right leg across his back letting myself down gently. I leaned down putting my head by his neck to steady myself. For a second everything was good, then my mind cleared. I know nothing about riding a horse, and when Mom and Dad find out, I will be grounded forever.

Halfway down the street, I realized we were moving. I held on with all I had. I laid my head against his neck, wrapped my fingers into his mane and pressed my legs against his body. The rhythm of my heart matched the rise and fall of his hooves. I was one with the horse.

We turned north on Forest Lane. Everything was normal until we were a half mile from my house. An empty field replaced the shopping center. Woods replaced houses. I held on with all my strength as we galloped across open fields. I trembled at the idea he was carrying me away from the life I knew, yet at the same time new strength, new life flowed from the horse into me. I shouted into the wind, "Ride, Henry ride." The horse went faster.

(I don't think I told you, my name is Henry. I'm named for a great grandfather who was an orphan. Sometimes I wish I was an orphan.)

The horse slowed to a walk. We stepped into the darkest darkness I ever experienced. My eyes were open, but I couldn't see anything. In the darkness, the horse, and I with him, made several very odd turns. At each turn I felt I was an image in a pop-up book being folded flat by the reader as they turned the page. Then on the next page I would rise up going in a new direction.

After the last turn, I rose up to the light of a new day. We were trotting down a mountain path. The mountain climbed up to my right and fell off sharply to my left. I leaned toward the mountain and away from the drop off. Occasionally, through the trees, I glimpsed lower hills and beyond them, a valley. The sun was at mid-morning, rising at the far end of the valley.

The horse stopped outside the ruins of a large stone building. I slipped off his back, though I more fell off than got off. When I returned to my feet, the horse was gone. I didn't have a clue where.

At this point in a movie, the main character always takes stock of the situation and so I took stock. I had no water, food, supplies or transportation, other than my feet. There is nothing like this building near my house. I concluded I am alone in an unknown land at some kind of ruin. (My life in middle school could be described as a ruin in an unknown land.)

My Dad has what he calls man rules. Man rule number five is, 'You have choices. You may not like your choices, but you have choices.' I had choices. Choice number one, I sit here and see what happens or choice number two, I get going and see what happens. You might be thinking how terribly brave I was, but at this point, a part of me believed this was a dream and if a dream, by waking up I would return to the safety of my bedroom. (The safety net would disappear shortly.)

I started walking around the building looking for a way in. I assumed I had arrived on the back side because there was no door and all the windows were high up in the wall. The wall towered two or more stories over me. Chunks of stone had fallen from above and lay on the ground along the base of the wall. As I came around the corner, I found a break in the wall and a pile of rubble below it. I managed to climb up the rubble and slip into the building through the crack. (Have I mentioned I am not the most athletic guy?)

I entered a large room the size of a gym. There were doors to other rooms. Even a second story, but the stairs lay collapsed on the floor. Large holes in the roof let in light. Someone or something had torn this place apart. Even parts of the floor had been pulled up. Almost immediately my skin began to crawl and the hair on my neck stood up. Outside there was a warm morning sun, but inside the building was cold and dark. The air was heavy and stale, like a wet basement. I had a bad feeling about the place. Something bad happened here. Something very bad happened here. Maybe worse, something bad was about to happen here. The feeling overwhelmed me and I tried to shake myself awake. (This is when I knew for certain I wasn't dreaming. I filled with fear and expectation.)

In the movies the characters always hang around in the bad place until something bad happens. It's called plot development. Not me, I headed for the largest opening to the outside. I had chosen the main entrance for my exit. Stone stairs led from this opening to a large courtyard below. Six smaller buildings made a semi-circle defining the area. They were messed up like the big building and some even had trees growing out of them.

Leaving the building did something for me. Inside me something more powerful than the bad of the building came alive. The new life the horse gave me lit a Fire deep inside me.

Once in gym, during track season, Coach yelled at me, "Miller, if you had a fire in your belly, you could jump those hurdles." I had no clue what he meant. I skipped lunch that day and all I had in my belly was bile. I caught my foot on the first hurdle and fell on my face. I crawled over to the side of the track with the dry heaves, but this is what he meant, this Fire in my gut quickly grew more powerful than the darkness of the building.

Standing at the doors of the building facing the courtyard, I raised my arms in a 'V,' as though pointing to the sky with two swords. I shouted at the top of my lungs,

"Good Bye, Henry of Suborediom.

I AM HENRY ON FIRE"

As I shouted, the Fire in me raged.

(This is what I am trying to tell you about, I want to hold on to this Fire.)

I started day dreaming about the life of Henry on Fire. I pictured the heroic Henry on Fire ruling over this place. I imagined people coming and going and doing everything I told them to do and asking me what they should do next. I was imagining ordering up lunch when an angry voice from behind me shocked me out of my day dream.

"Where do you come from? No one is allowed here."

Out of reflex or from watching too many old movies, I raised my hands and turned around slowly. The voice belonged to an old guy with a wispy beard and dressed in a dingy gray robe. I've had a growth spurt and he was old and shrunken so I was almost as tall as him. The difference was he was shaking a stick at me, six inches in front of my face. I couldn't tell if he was shaking because of rage or age. I froze.

"Account for yourself, boy."

My voice caught in my throat, but I managed to say, "I'm not doing anything. I didn't mess with anything or touch anything. I found the place like this."

He growled, "Where do you come from?"

I should have said, 'I come from my Mother's womb, where did you come from' or even 'I come from 10510 Timber Lane in Suborediom.' I chose a cautious answer, "I came down the mountain."

After a long pause, during which he carefully looked me over, he lowered his stick and walked past me, out into the court yard, saying nothing. I hate it when adults treat me that way. When he had gone thirty feet he turned back, I guess to see if I would follow him.

7

The smart move would be to take off running, circle around the building and head back out on the trail I came in on. But that road leads to Suborediom and suffocation. No today the horse gave me the chance to choose a new road and the Fire in me gave me the courage to take the new road.

I followed the old man through the courtyard and onto a trail into the woods. We came to his camp at a clearing a hundred yards in. I stopped at a small fire at the center of the camp. The old man headed into a shack off to one side of the clearing. Still not looking back at me or saying a word. He returned with some bread, cheese and some other things.

I sat down and started to eat, the bread was dry and the cheese smelled like gym socks. Fortunately he brought me a cup of cold water which helped me wash both down. I ate because I was hungry. He sat across the fire from me. He started stirring up the fire and adding stuff to a cooking pot. Every so often he would stop and stare at me like I had two heads. I didn't like it.

Finally he asked, I guess he more demanded, "What brings you to Lothar?"

His abruptness caught me off guard, "Pardon?"

"Lothar, the name of the house is Lothar," he said a little less roughly.

"Yes, Lothar, I came to look around." I wanted him to think I knew where I was. I started to think of the conversation as a chess game and thought I should take control of the board. (I play chess at lunch every day with Fred and Jamal.)

I stood up and poured on the manners saying, "I am quite sorry sir, I came uninvited to your home and I have not even introduced myself. My name is Henry." I couldn't decide whether to extend my hand for a handshake or bow or what to do. It didn't matter because the old man just sat there. I gave an awkward bow and sat back down. (So much for opening moves.)

"Henry." He said my name as if tasting the word. He said it again, "Henry," into the air, as if he needed to hear the sound of it. It was weird. After a long silence he said, "I am mostly called Papo, or old man, but my name is Alrinar."

I took some more bread and cheese. I chewed slowly in order to buy some time. I finally asked, "How long has Lothar been abandoned?"

"The Taking happened at last night's moon, a hundred years ago. The Tara ordered every stone and timber searched and when the child was not found, he turned his back on Lothar. He forbade any to return."

"And you, why are you here?"

Papo studied my face as if he was trying to remember something. "I come every fall, in case the child returns."

I laughed, coughed and blew water out my nose. As I recovered, I blurted out, "That would be a really old child by now." But at the same time the Fire in my gut grew stronger.

He smiled at my outburst and said, "Maybe."

"And you, have you been coming here for a hundred years?"

"I'm old but not that old. I've been coming for many years."

Something changed in the old man's face during this conversation. He acted warmer towards me, but with the kind of friendliness that is fake or even creepy. He began to volunteer information. "A few families live to the north, in the mountains and beyond, but we rarely have contact with them. Maybe you have been there?"

"I have been to the north of here." I technically did not lie, because as best I could tell the trail I came in on was north of the camp.

"The land of Altara stretches east from the mountains. The land follows the valley of the river Al. Most people live in five villages along the river, Para, Nork, Tran, Roan and Rahtol. The last village, Rahtol, is on an island where the river meets the sea. Perhaps you have been to the sea?"

"I have been to the sea." Again technically I didn't lie. We go to the ocean once a year. I just doubt I have been to his sea.

"The valley of the river Al is the land of the Tara." As he talked, he seemed less creepy and more just boring.

"And the Tara, who is he?" I asked.

"The Tara was once a powerful leader. The last true Tara built Lothar, but after the Taking, the rights of the Tara passed to the son of a brother and now, for several generations we haven't had a true Tara. Now we are to claim that a boy of no more than thirteen years is the Tara." His voice grew angry as he mentioned the boy.

"Tell me the story of the Taking. What's that about?"

"Look at the sun, it's getting late and we have things to do before dark, that story is a hundred

10

years old, it will keep a while longer." As he finished saying this he got up and headed over to his hut. He came back with a bucket. Pointing to the side of camp opposite where we came in he said, "There's a trail that heads out that side of the camp, at the end of the trail you'll find a spring. Fill this bucket and come back."

I just stood there looking at the guy. Who is he to assign me chores? I guess he understood the look.

He said, "Camp doesn't run on its own. If you want some dinner and want water to wash up, you need to pitch in."

I took the bucket and headed down the trail. (I find myself in some alternate world and an adult is assigning me chores. Really!) The path went on forever, heading down hill. The spring bubbled out of a pile of rocks into a shallow pool about three feet in diameter. The water was cold and clear. I filled the bucket. As I headed back uphill, the daylight faded fast and I had to work hard to follow the trail and to not spill too much water. The whole trip took about an hour. I was relieved to see the fire of camp through the trees.

As soon as I came into camp, Papo greeted me, "Well there you are. I thought maybe you lost your way." He sounded sincerely concerned. He took the bucket, poured water in a bowl and rinsed his face and hands. I did likewise.

All day I had only eaten the biscuit and cheese Papo gave me. I was definitely hungry. We sat down at the fire and Papo handed me a wooden bowl of the stew he had been working on in the pot. I ate with a wooden spoon. If cafeteria food is your standard, this scored above average for taste and smell. As we finished our food Papo asked, "Inside or out?"

"What?"

"Do you want to sleep inside or outside?" he asked.

"I'm not planning on staying," I said. I figured I ought to be getting home. Between the ride and spending the day in Altara, I was sure everyone would be looking for me. A wave of guilt, fear and regret swept over me. I knew I faced a magnitude of trouble and disbelief as soon as I got home.

"Where would you be going?" he asked.

"Well, that is a good question," I looked around and realized it was now pitch dark beyond the light of the fire. I doubt I could even find my way back to Lothar much less the trail I came in on. So I started thinking about whether to choose inside or outside. In the hut I would be safe from whatever goes bumping around outside in the dark. (This is not Suborediom.) But I would not be safe from this old guy, who I only just met. Also, if I was outside and I stayed awake, the horse might come back for me.

"Outside," I said. Papo handed me a mat and some rough blankets, and I set them up as a bed at the edge of the fire. As I lay down, I asked, "How about the story of the Taking before I go to sleep."

"No, I will tell you that story tomorrow. After that though I am heading down the mountain and going on to Para. You are welcome to come," he said as he went into his hut.

I tried to stay awake to wait for the horse, but in truth, I was exhausted and went right to sleep. I

woke at seven this morning in my own bed trying
to make sense of what happened during the night.

☐

Chapter 2 Monday in Suborediom

I have more to tell you about Altara, but I need to clear my head about school today, especially gym class. My life is changing everywhere.

I got to the bus stop early, because I wanted to tell Fred about the horse and Lothar and Papo. I was still Henry on Fire. I started by saying, "I went to another world last night."

Before I added anything, Fred said, "I believe another Earth of the exact same size as our Earth orbits on the opposite side of the sun, spinning in the opposite direction. Everything in that world is opposite. They call it Htrae and there Jamal is captain of the football team and you are the quarterback and I am the field goal kicker. Every Friday night when I come out to kick the winning goal, the announcer says, 'Here's Fabulous Fred the Fearless Field Goal Fellow.' And then I kick the winning goal."

"Don't I have a nickname like high flying Henry?"

"No, I don't think you do."

We were at school and I didn't have a chance to tell him about Altara. At least Fred made room for Jamal and me in his day dream. Sometimes I think Fred and I are only friends because we live across the street and we share the lower rungs of the middle school social ladder. Jamal hangs with us because I help him with math and we all like to play chess. And as long as I'm being honest, I think playing chess at lunch is a way to cover for our lack of social skills. I don't want to be class president or Mr. Popular, I just want to be average, maybe with a girlfriend and more than two people to talk to in the halls.

Anyway, I need to tell you what happened in gym class. We were suited up, and sitting in our squad lines on the floor with our legs crossed.

Coach Thompson pulled on the rope hanging from the ceiling and announced to us, "By the end of next week every one of you is going to climb this rope."

I leaned over to Fred and whispered, "I'll climb that rope the day the Troglodyte plays a decent game of chess."

Fred laughed. The day we learned the word, troglodyte (any caveman), we immediately began to use it as our nickname for Coach.

Well, Coach caught us cutting up and I guess he heard me, though he was thirty feet away. He strolled down our line towards me. The gym grew silent. Everyone in middle school fears Coach. I could feel a death sentence headed my way or at least a detention.

He bent down, looked me right in the face, and in an almost friendly voice said, "Well, Miller, let's have a little wager? I'll join your chess group at lunch tomorrow, and if I make a decent showing, you climb halfway up the rope, and if I win, you climb all the way up the rope!"

His friendliness was more shocking than if he had yelled at me. Doing my best to hold myself together (I had no Fire left in me), and shaking in my voice, I managed to say, "If I win, what then?"

Coach replied, "No rope."

Gaining courage I added, "What about Fred?"

"No rope for Fred either."

He agreed to the chess match with such confidence, I thought he might actually know how to play. The idea devastated me.

On the bus ride home, Fred wanted to talk about strategies for the chess match. Jamal isn't taking gym this semester. Fred and I have a lot riding on the match. I doubt either of us can climb even a fourth of the way up the rope.

When I got home, I had chores. Today was dusting. I hate dusting. Last year I had to go to the end of our street every day at four, to walk Larry home from the bus stop, but now he is in fourth grade and he walks himself home. After chores I went to my room to write. (Thanks for sticking with me.)

Today was Monday, so we ate at the table. It's okay. We had the usual conversations about 'What happened at school today?' I usually choose one thing to share. Luckily, Larry talks a lot and fills the time. Dad reports on the people in his carpool. When he does talk about his work, we don't understand. He's a software development engineer who devises new codes for communication applications. (He made me memorize that because he says, 'A boy ought to be able to tell people what his father does.' Nobody ever asks.) Mom works at the library and she talks about new books.

Unexpectedly, half way through the meal, Mom turned to me and said, "Oh, Henry, I forgot to get a book on dreams, but tell us your dream."

"What?" I had forgotten that at breakfast I mentioned I dreamed all night I was somewhere else.

"This morning you said you had a very real dream. What was it about?" Larry and Dad were also looking at me.

I didn't want to share a story that started with, 'I slipped out the front door last night,' so I tried to deflect. "I went to the library during lunch and researched dreams on Wikipedia. The article said you should write down your dreams, so I'm going to do that right after I finish my homework."

As I hoped, Dad jumped on the mention of Wikipedia, "I was at a programming conference in Los Angeles and just having drinks after the conference and I told this guy about my idea for an online encyclopedia to collect knowledge from all over the globe. I was going to call it Knowledgemania. Anyway, not two years later, Wikipedia comes rolling out. Life would have been different if I hadn't given that idea away." I just sat quietly through the rest of dinner.

I was in bed at nine thirty, hoping the horse would come back. I was still awake, reading, when my parents went to bed at ten. I wanted to go back to Altara to be Henry on Fire and to get Papo to tell me the story of the Taking. Also I had been thinking about the boy Tara all day. I'm thirteen and I don't think I'm a kid anymore. The world outside my window was quiet Suborediom. I fell asleep shortly after eleven. I woke up in Altara.

Chapter 3 A Second Day in Altara

I woke by the fire in Papo's camp. (I can only tell you what happened, I can't tell you why it happened this way, but I do have a theory. I think the horse came to find me and in doing so, created a link between our two worlds. So when I'm asleep in one world, I'm awake in the other. I wonder why the horse came for me.) Even though I went to sleep in my bed, I was sore from sleeping on the ground in Altara. My Fire was back and I felt Altara was where I was supposed to be.

Papo came out of the hut. "Rather a late sleeper, aren't you? The day is already a couple of hours gone. That's okay, we still have time to make it to the bottom of the mountain. If you are coming."

"What about breakfast?" I asked, speaking for my growling stomach.

"A biscuit and bark tea is all I have to offer. This is the last day of camp and I put everything edible in last night's stew." He handed me the biscuit and tea.

My stomach turned a little, wondering what I ate last night. The biscuit was even harder and drier than the bread yesterday. The bark tea was something between coffee and tea. I dunked the biscuit in the tea and manage to eat it. As I chewed it down, I asked, "What about the story of the Taking."

"We need to break camp first and get moving."

What an adult! I can't believe there are more chores. Chores always come first for adults.

Papo assigned putting out the fire to me. Fortunately we had leftover water from yesterday's trip to the spring. I stirred the water into the coals until they stopped smoking. He gathered up some things from around the camp and put them in the hut. He put a brace against the door of the hut to block it shut. He gave me a large long-sleeve hooded shirt. He said it would be better for walking through the woods. The shirt swallowed me, but I agreed to wear it. We each took a bag with a strap. I slung mine over my shoulder, pony express style. The bag had more biscuits, a skin water bag, and my sleeping mat.

We left the camp and headed up towards Lothar. We stopped near the cluster of buildings on the left side of the courtyard. Papo began, "This was the camp of the hunters. The story begins here." The following is the story of the Taking as told by Papo.

On the last day of the season, the Tara called together all the men and women at Lothar. Before the whole gathering, he gave to his son, Anree, the key to the gates of Altara. He declared Anree, Master of the Gate. Anree was no older than thirteen, but the Tara was telling the people, 'My son will be the next Tara.' He placed the key on a leather strap and hung it on Anree's neck. The people all cheered and spent the rest of the day in feasting and games.

Late in the night when most had gone to sleep, a party was still underway in the court of the hunters. People were in a large circle around a bonfire. Occasionally a group would get up and dance or start hunting calls. Then, a unicorn leapt into the center of the circle. The creature of legend was real!

The hunters jumped to their feet. Someone shouted, "Close the circle. Get ropes." They raised their arms with burning sticks to keep the animal from jumping over them or running through their circle. People tried to lasso the animal. The animal rose up on its hind legs, kicking at them, then down again as if it would charge them with its horn.

Shouting and hollering they tightened their circle around the creature. Suddenly, the heavens broke with the loudest thunder ever heard. The shock of the thunder silenced the whole gathering. The sky opened and rain poured down so hard, streams of water rushed through the camp, putting out the fires and knocking down tents. The circle broke apart and the unicorn ran up toward the main house. Some claimed lightening ran from the top of the mountain to the sky. Running wildly up toward the big house, the unicorn must have run into a rock out cropping and broke off its horn. (Papo points to the likely rock.) One of the men kept the horn.

As quickly as the torrents of rain came, they passed, leaving only a dark night and a light misty drizzle. The camp grew quiet as people tried to find a dry place to sleep.

An hour later the whole encampment awoke to cries of alarm from the main house. The child, Anree, was missing. Everyone searched for the child. The mountain glowed with torches as people searched and called for Anree. They searched through the night.

In the morning, they began again. The Tara ordered every room, building and tent searched. Anree was still not found and the Tara ordered the buildings to be pulled apart in search of hiding places. For days they searched the mountain and tore the buildings apart. Some began to say Anree had ridden the lightening up into the sky. Others said the unicorn took the boy. After twelve days, the Tara and all the people turned their back on Lothar and went down the mountain.

Neither the child, nor any trace of the child, was ever found. The Tara forbade anyone to ever return to Lothar. The rights of the Tara passed to a nephew. The gates of Altara have not been opened, and the unicorn has not been seen in the land since.

When he finished, we started our journey down the mountain. The Fire had returned and told me this was the right way to be going. The path was once the main road up to Lothar. It was wide enough for two horses to walk side by side.

"So what happened to the boy," I asked.

Papo shrugs his shoulders.

I clearly understand now why my Dad gets so annoyed when I answer a question with a shrug.

"Okay, so do you think the unicorn took the boy or do you think the boy rode the lightning into the sky?" I thought he might do better with a multiple choice question.

"To be honest I don't think it matters, I think the point is the boy is gone."

"Who took the horn?" I asked.

"What?"

"Who took the unicorn horn?" I asked again. This seemed like an important detail to me. One of Fred's Dads is a hunter and he has antlers all over the garage walls. I would think someone would keep a unicorn horn. (People always want to know how Fred has two dads. He could have a real dad and a step dad, he could have two step dads, or his mother could have two husbands but really his dads are gay and it's okay.)

"The story is old, who knows, the story is about why the Tara is not a real Tara. The story tells us the true Tara was taken from us. The unicorn is the symbol of the mystery, a symbol of the unknown person who took the boy."

All I could think was 'with explanations like that, this guy ought to teach English classes.' I wasn't happy with his answers to my questions, but I let it go. The Fire in my gut was telling me that whatever I'm after is down the mountain and that was where we were heading.

After a while we left the main road for what Papo called a short cut. The trail narrowed and became more difficult. On the short cut we climbed up several smaller mountains in order to go down the big mountain. (This didn't make any sense to me.) When we reached the top of each hill, we took a short break. Papo explained that the road is a gentler trip around the mountain, but takes a full day to reach the bottom. Since we left Lothar at midmorning, this short cut would get us to the bottom before dark.

Papo was rather sure-footed for an old guy. The trail in some places was solid rock and in other places loose gravel. For me the solid rock parts caused difficulty when we were going uphill and the loose gravel proved treacherous on downhill portions of the trail. In fact, one time my feet slipped out from under me and I had to grab a tree to keep from going down the side of the mountain on my butt.

I am not a total couch potato, but I am also definitely not a hiker or a camper. This is my way of telling you the newness, of this down-the-mountain trip, wore off pretty quickly and was on its way to being hard work.

As we got near the bottom of the mountain and the path got easier, Papo struck up a conversation. "We are going to meet some people down here. They are rather wild people."

"Why do we want to meet up with wild people?" I asked.

"They will protect us from dangerous animals as we cross the grasslands, but you must remember they are not to be trusted."

"What do you mean not trusted?"

"They live mostly out here in the wild. They are as dangerous as the animals they are hired to protect us from. When they do come into the village, mothers make their children go inside. I am a bit worried about them seeing you," he said.

"Well I forgot to pack my invisibility cloak, so I don't think I can avoid being seen. And if they see me, what are they going to do?"

He ignored my invisibility cloak comment and said, "If they think you're an orphan boy..."

23

The Fire inside me raged when he called me an 'orphan boy.' I abruptly interrupted him shouting, "I never said I'm an orphan." Everything about this bothered me and especially being called an 'orphan boy.' (Yes, I said earlier that sometimes I wish I was an orphan. So I don't know what I want, I'm thirteen, can't you cut me some slack. I know I sound mad, but this really upset me.)

He tried to calm me down saying, "Okay, if they think you are a boy alone in the land, they will want me to give you to them as payment for their troubles and then they will sell you to someone else."

"Really?" I said, "So how about we skip them and take our chances crossing the grasslands by ourselves."

"No," he said, "Here's my plan. Keep the hood on the shirt I gave you up over your head so they can't see your face. I'll tell them you're an older relative from up in the mountains. And if they ask you something nod or give them a short yes or no or make a gesture with your hand."

I had my doubts about something in the story of the Taking, but now I had even more doubts. Yet I did as Papo suggested. The trail led right into the camp. The camp had four lean-tos arranged around a fire in the center.

Our grassland guides were three men and three women. On first impression they didn't seem dangerous. They asked questions about me, but they quickly seemed to accept Papo's story. As the evening went on, I realized Papo must have planned to return today, even before he met me, or else how would they have known to be here today. I didn't know if this meant anything.

We ate around the fire. They tried to get Papo to talk about his time up the mountain and the condition of Lothar, but he wouldn't share anything. Then they tried to talk to me, but I waved off their conversation and Papo made some excuse for my silence. For the rest of the evening, I sat listening to them retelling stories of their hunts. They were three couples, Shara and Ra, Yat and Evra, Kur and Lara. The men were mainly spear hunters. The women were mainly bow hunters. They all had large knives.

In some ways Shara seems to lead, because, according to their stories, she is the best tracker. Ra and Yat are the most skilled at slipping up silently on prey. I could tell they were a team that functions as one. (Another sports concept I never seem to succeed at.) Nothing they said sounded at all false, or implied they had a going trade in 'orphan boys.'

At the end of the evening, Papo and I retired to the fourth lean-to. Papo put himself between the rest of the group and me. I found it much harder to fall asleep on the ground tonight as images of a trade in 'orphan boys' played through my mind.

Chapter 4 Tuesday at School
The Chess Match

On the bus this morning, I had all kind of things from last night racing around in my head, but Fred wanted to talk about the chess game. He and Jamal stayed up late discussing strategies for my match with Coach. Fred repeated the full discussion to me. I didn't pay any attention until he said, "You have to sit on the east side of the board."

"What?" I asked.

"East, sit on the east side of the board," he repeated as though this was common knowledge for anyone who plays chess.

I knew I wasn't ready for the answer, but I asked, "Why?"

"I found a blog last night called, 'Chess, the Winner's Secrets' and he analyzed all the records of tournament play for the past twenty years. The player on the east side of the board won 5% more often than the player on the west side of the board." Fred said this with all sincerity. He just wanted to help because he has no better chance at climbing the rope than I do.

"Really," I'm holding back a laugh and trying to appreciate his help.

"Yes, really, somehow it's a home field advantage."

As we got off the bus, I told Fred, "I'm pretty sure the tables in the cafeteria run east and west, so I'll have to sit on the north or south side. What should I do?"

Without even pausing, he said, "Definitely the south side, the blog says that is the second most advantageous position."

I headed for my locker.

During my morning classes, I tried to focus on my chess strategy, but the teachers had their own plans for how to spend my time at school. Whenever I passed Fred or Jamal in the hall, they had more chess game advice which made my stomach tighten into one giant knot. I tried to get the Fire in my gut going to drive my game forward, but I couldn't build a connection between Henry on Fire and school.

I arrived at the lunch table before coach. I hoped he wouldn't show, but he came a few minutes later. Once he sat down, our table became the center of attention. We flipped a coin to decide who opened. Jamal brought a timer and we agreed to a twenty-five minute game. Jamal also brought several different sets of tournament rules and wanted to serve as referee for the game. We told him we were playing a friendly game and didn't need to get overly technical. Fred brought an onyx chess set.

I won the toss and opened with my queen's pawn. (I sat on the south side of the table.) Coach responded by bringing out his knight. I planned to establish control of the center of the board. For my second move, I brought out my knight. Now the crowd grew to five deep with people standing on chairs to watch. Everyone had opinions about the next move, including someone behind me who said, "What chess needs is a ninja warrior."

We were only four moves into the game, when Fred, Jamal and I realized he was a formidable opponent. I asked, "So Coach, where did you learn to play chess?"

"Well you might be surprised to learn, I was president of my high school chess club."

I think two of the football players and Fred fainted at this announcement.

On his fifth move, he castled his king, moving the piece to the corner under the protection of his rook. I thought it was a little early for that move. I guess he saw the questioning look on my face. "Chess taught me to think ahead. Not to just play, but to play with a strategy."

The crowd had thinned by now, after all, chess is not an action sport.

On my seventh move, I took his pawn, the first kill of the game. The remaining crowd erupted in a cheer as if I had made a touchdown. Some of the crowd returned. My Fire came back to me. Then Mr. Rhoads, the assistant principal, showed up saying, "Break it up. Break it up. What's going on here?" And even though I was sitting with Coach, I got a sinking feeling like I was in trouble.

However, when he finally discovered Coach, me and a chess game at the center of the crowd, everything was okay, but he told the guys not to stand on the chairs.

Coach told the crowd, "Chess is not a basketball game, it's a game of strategy and the crowd needs to be a little more respectful."

People in the crowd started saying things like, "Okay," "Sure," "Whatever," "Get the dweeb," and a muffled, "Slaughter the Troglodyte."

Coach looked at me, "Troglodyte?"

My face turned bright red, but with as honest of a voice as possible, I lied, "I have no idea what they meant."

Coach laughed.

Working hard to not sound nervous I said, "I don't know anyone who is a troglodyte."

Coach said, "I don't know anyone who is a dweeb."

On his thirteenth move, he pulled his queen back and I realized he had no pieces beyond his third row and I had none past the center of the board. He was playing much less aggressively than we do, but his strategy was much stronger than mine. I concentrated on understanding his plan of attack. Four moves later, he fully re-engaged my men and had both my bishops under threat. Any retaliation would cost me the avenging piece, any withdrawal, would lead to further exposure. Move nineteen I took his knight, he took my bishop. Only a small crowd remained to cheer. The bell rang, ending lunch. In the final moves, he took my knight and I took his bishop. (Move 25)

We had the same pieces on the board, but their positioning definitely gave him an advantage. I would be playing a defensive game from here on out and unless he made a mistake, he would win. I don't think he would have made a mistake.

As we stood up we had only a dozen or so observers. They were a mix of sports kids, cool kids, Fred and Jamal. I extended my hand, and while looking him in the eye said, "I will do everything I can to climb the rope."

Coach said, "I'll sign on as faculty sponsor for a chess club."

Fred standing beside me whispered, "I'll never be able to climb the rope. You should have sat on the east side. We could have turned the tables around."

The afternoon was a whole new world. News of the chess match spread through school and everyone was talking about it. Fred, Jamal and I moved up from the bottom, not far up from the bottom, but up from the bottom. People, okay, only two people, but two people, who had never spoken to me before, acknowledged my existence. I was on Fire.

During the chess game, I learned from Coach that I need a strategy for school. I have been letting life assign me to dweeb status. I need to decide who I am. I need a strategy. I need to say, "Hello, I am Henry. Deal with me." Maybe "Hello, I'm Henry on Fire, respect me." But in chess and life, there is a world of difference between learning a strategy from a book and using it while in play. First I need to figure out how to be Henry on Fire, alive in Suborediom.

When I got home today, my chore was bringing in the trashcans and recycling bins. Dad puts them out in the morning on his way to work. I bring them in when I get off the bus after school. Larry does nothing. I decided I need some muscles to get up the rope, so I found a piece of pipe in the garage. I mounted it between the fence and the back wall of the garage as a chin up bar. After I set it in place and put Dad's tools away, I started to go in. As I got to the back door, I realized the bar would do no good if I didn't actually do a chin up. I did one and a half. It's going to be a long way up that rope. I went to bed early.

Chapter 5 The Grasslands of Altara

I woke in the camp on the mat where I went to sleep. Everyone else was already moving around. I sat up without the hood hiding my face. Papo freaked out trying to cover my head before anyone noticed.

I had a good feeling about these people. I don't believe these people would sell me into slavery, not that I have ever met any slave traders. My Dad threatens to give me away, but then he laughs and says now that I am a teenager, no one will take me. (It's a dumb joke.) The more time I spent with the guides, the more I believed the hood disguise served some other purpose.

Breakfast this morning included some berries Kur brought in and some fish Ra speared in a nearby stream. We ate breakfast, gathered our stuff and then, before we put out the fire, everyone threw on a handful of grass.

Shara speaking to the group, but probably for my benefit said, "We cast our hope upon the fire, asking the wind to guide our journey through the grasslands and return us to our Mother, the river Al."

After thirty minutes of walking, we left the mountains and trees behind. A grass covered plain stretched before us all the way to the horizon.

The guides spread out walking in a wide arc, each twenty feet from the next. Papo explained, "They are watching for cats hiding in the grass. If we walked in a line as on a trail, a cat might attack the first or more likely the last person and the others would not be able to help as quickly. The

32

grass hides the cats, but also feeds the antelope. We cast the grass on the fire as a symbol of our hope to pass through safely."

While Papo talked about symbols and stuff, I hoped to see one of these cats. Would they be more like lions or house cats or maybe a saber tooth tiger?

In the thick tall grass, the guides stayed on high alert, but in places with thinner and shorter grass, everyone relaxed. We entered a large area of low grass and I found myself walking near Shara. Ra was involving Papo in a discussion and slowly moving him away from me.

This seemed fine because I had taken a liking to Shara. She couldn't be more than five or six years older than me and I can only say, I had never been this close to such a healthy woman. (Okay, I'm trying to be polite. What if my mom reads this? The word I am looking for is somewhere between gorgeous and so hot she made me sweat.)

She spoke in a strikingly soft voice, "Have you known Papo long?"

I gave a simple and honest, "No."

"Is your home far from here?"

"Yes, I come from far away, very far," again being truthful.

My mind raced to try to understand why I cautiously answered all Papo's question and now to Shara, I kept telling the truth. Does she have reason to ask these questions or is she just curious? After all if they did want to sell me into slavery, they needed to find out if anyone would come looking for me. I feared I would answer any question she asked.

Ra continued to keep Papo distracted and actually everyone had worked together to gradually change positions as we walked, creating a greater distance between Papo and myself. Animal Planet shows how the lions work together to isolate an animal from its herd before they pounce on it. These guides were setting their trap for me.

Shara picked back up her inquiry, "Do you know where Papo is taking you?"

I remained silent. We set out with the guides for Para, but I did not have a clue what Papo planned beyond Para. I was following the Fire in my gut, but I didn't want to try to explain the Fire to Shara. She knew my silence meant I couldn't answer her question.

She continued, "We have a saying, if you do not lead yourself, you will surely be led by another."

Her words meant I had surrendered myself to Papo without knowing anything about him. I felt like I had been pounced upon. Then, as if her words weren't pointed enough, in one fast graceful move she, pulled her knife from its place on her ankle and threw it into the ground a few feet in front of me. I gasped thinking this was a threat or warning to me. The others gathered around, knives drawn and spears raised. Yat smiled and casually pulled the knife from the ground. Along with the knife came a four foot snake. The knife had gone right through its head. Yat said, "Deadly." I wondered if he meant the snake or Shara's knife.

Papo realized how far I had strayed and was now back at my side. I had no Fire in me. I let Papo lead me through Altara like I let people lead

34

me through my life in Suborediom. I need to get out in front of my life. I need to lead Henry. I believe the horse intentionally brought me here. I believe Henry on Fire has a job to do here. I realized again, I have choices. I can stay with Papo or I can cast my lot with the guides. Shara may be warning me about Papo or she might be trying to cause me to doubt Papo for a purpose of her own. I didn't need to decide then but a time for a decision would come.

We chewed on some type of jerky for lunch.

By mid-afternoon I was hot and sweaty under the hood and long sleeves. I wanted to ditch the shirt. Obviously Papo benefitted from me wearing the shirt, but what if the disguise also benefited me. I went back and forth in my mind trying to decide if the guides or Papo were the bad guys. I don't believe Papo has been truthful to me, but I also have not been fully truthful either. Overall he has been good to me. I thought what if they are all bad guys, maybe I need to set out on my own following the Fire. I kept the shirt on and sweated.

A group of trees appeared in the distance, fortunately right in our path. Shara indicated the trees and announced, mostly to me, "The Well of the Wind."

We entered the grove cautiously, checking for wild animals. Several dozen trees surrounded a spring fed pool.

Shara led the way in, checking for wildlife, and then announced, "If we rest here for two hours, we can still make Para before sunset and our old traveler will not be so tired." She said this looking at me, not Papo. We each refilled our water bottles in the pool and splashed cool water on our faces.

After freshening up I started to settle down at the foot of a tree. Yat shook his head no, "That's a good place to rest if you want to be eaten by a cat coming for a drink of water."

Ra and Shara were already climbing into a tree. Shara grabbed a limb four feet above her head and swung her legs up with the ease of a trapeze artist. She reached down and pulled Ra up to the branch. Once he grabbed hold of the branch, he easily swung his legs up. Yat and Evra followed Shara and Ra up into the tree.

Kar, Lara and Papo went up another tree in a similar manner. I followed, but even with Kar's help climbing into the tree took every bit of strength I had. Kar's help also meant he looked me straight in my face as he reached down for my hand and I reached up. He smiled when he saw my face.

Anyway, if climbing this tree was so hard, how hard will the rope be to climb next week? We continued to climb farther up into the tree. Thirty feet above the ground, there were several places where a webbing of rope had been strung between the branches, creating stationary hammocks. They reminded me of the baskets on the end of a lacrosse stick, only big enough for a person. We each settled into one. Everyone seemed to be planning on an afternoon nap. I wondered what would happen if I fell asleep.

I watched the watering hole through the webbing. Fifteen minutes after we settled into our 'nests' two antelopes came to the edge of the pool to drink. When they finished, they slipped away into the tall grass as silently as they arrived.

No more than ten minutes later, a large cat came to the edge of the pool to drink. The cat was proportioned like a short hair house cat, but stood as tall as a large dog. It was dark tan in color with a light streak down the ridge of its back. From my safe perch high above, the animal looked powerful, but not particularly threatening. I wondered if it could climb trees. It also left silently.

I fell asleep and awoke in my own bed. My alarm clock read three-thirty. My room was dark, the house quiet and the street outside, silent and deserted.

If you are wondering, this waking up in different places gets confusing. I started to call my Dad, Papo, yesterday. Writing helps keep things straight in my mind, but it's not necessary, because none of this disappears from my memory. My memory of walking around Lothar Sunday night is as clear as my memory of walking into school Monday morning.

I took an hour to fall back asleep.

When I woke back in Altara, everyone was stirring. The other four were already down from their tree. They helped Papo down from our tree. I dropped to the ground without a problem. Shara was looking at me as I landed. I wondered if Kar had already reported looking at my face as I climbed up into the tree.

The rest did me well and the day was starting to cool down. Papo kept me close by his side.

As we walked along I asked, "So, after Para, where are we going?"

"I've been wondering when you would ask," he said. "I thought we would stay a day or two in Para and then go by boat with everyone else to the Gathering. I have some friends to meet before we leave Para."

"Friends?" I ask.

"Oh, they're acquaintances. I just need to say hello."

For the next two hours until we reached the river the Fire simmered within me. Something in the word 'friends' did not sit well with me.

At the river, each of the guides knelt and drank, bending to the water with their faces. Papo did likewise, so I followed suit. Shara looked at me and said, "We are blessed to drink again of the water of the Al. We trust in the river to nourish the land and restore our souls."

Para lay a hundred yards across the river from us and a boat was already coming to ferry us over. As the boat neared, Papo gave each of our guides a coin and thanked them for their assistance.

Yat asked, "Do you want us again next year?"

Papo replied, "No, I won't be going to Lothar next year."

The Fire flared in my gut. This guy thinks I'm the child that was taken and has now returned. This makes no sense. He is one confused old guy. I am ready to hitch on with the guides, but what happens if they don't want me?

When the boat came to the shore, the guides climbed in first.

Papo was surprised, "You're going to Para?"

Yat replied, "We thought we would lay over in Para for a day or two and then go by boat to the Gathering."

Papo replied with a tone of amazement, "You're going to the Gathering."

Yat spoke again, "We will pledge ourselves to the new Tara."

Papo didn't care for this news. I was glad. We followed the guides into the boat. When we exited the ferry, we parted company with the guides, but I took comfort in them still being in the area. At least a hundred boats lined the river shore at Para. Some floated in the river. Some were drawn up on the shore. The boats were twenty to thirty feet long and six and ten feet wide, with a small cabin at the center. A small mast at the center above the cabin provided a place for a sail. We arrived at dusk, so I could not see much of the village.

Papo lead me down the shore to a boat I assumed was his. The boat was floating in the river, but tied to a post at the shore. He pulled it in and we climbed aboard. Furs and blankets covered the floor area of the cabin. This would definitely be my most comfortable sleeping experience in Altara.

Papo said he was going for some food and left me in the boat. I could hear people in other boats nearby, but in the darkness I couldn't see anyone. I laid down on some blankets in the bow of the boat. The stars filled the sky above me from one horizon to the other. I can name a few major constellations like the Big Dipper, and the Little Dipper, but I couldn't find them among so many stars. I fell asleep beneath that amazing sky.

Chapter 6 Wednesday Morning
Stolen Fire

This morning on the bus, Fred kept talking about yesterday's science class. Mrs. Ridley spent the whole hour on continental drift and how it related to earthquakes and volcanoes in the Pacific ring of fire. She showed a video of the one giant land mass, called Pangaea, breaking apart into our modern world. She even played the video backwards and they went back together like a jigsaw puzzle.

Fred said, "I believe there were people in Pangaea 450 million years ago. People like us, and whatever broke up Pangaea into the seven continents totally wiped out everything they built. Life restarted because some of their DNA survived."

"Wow, Fred that is your wildest idea ever." Yet for a few moments, I thought this idea could explain Altara. Even if only for a moment, I liked having an explanation.

I walked into school feeling the Fire within me. Yesterday's chess match opened such possibilities and I actually enjoyed talking to Coach. I smiled and nodded at people. Tervel and Dante joined our lunch table. Tervel says he's named for a football player and Dante says he never heard of the Inferno. In just one day, I was becoming the person I wanted to be.

After lunch I stopped at my locker to put away my chess set and get my afternoon books. I nodded to Rick whose locker is near mine. Rick and I went to elementary school together, but we have never been friends.

Rick thinks he's a tough guy. He hangs around with a few other tough guy types. They don't do sports and they don't fit in any better than Fred, Jamal and I, but tough seems cooler. Well as Rick left his locker, I bent down to pick up my books off the floor, and Rick slammed my locker shut. He looked at me and said, "You're still a dweeb with a chess board." My Fire went out. I stared at him. I wanted to say, 'You're just a thug without a chess board,' but I didn't.

I can't decide whether Rick stole my Fire or I let him take away my Fire. Shara said last night, 'If you do not lead yourself, you will surely be led by another.' If I let people take my Fire aren't I letting them lead me? If I let people label me a dweeb, aren't I letting them be in charge of my life? Still, I was bummed out.

After supper I worked on geometry for an hour. Jamal and I played online chess at eight. I haven't told Fred or Jamal or anyone about Altara and, as I finish each day's journal pages, I add them to a notebook I'm keeping in my desk drawer.

Chapter 7 A Day in Para

The day started off nicely. I slept far better in the boat than on the ground. Papo was still asleep when I woke. I flipped the hood up over my head as I stood to take a look around. I acknowledged people on the nearby boats with a wave. I breathed deeply, taking in the air and the sky and the river. They all calmed me. I thought I had been too suspicious of Papo.

Turning from the river, I got my first good look at the town. Wood and plaster buildings surrounded a large open area where people were unloading carts and wagons for a market. I noticed there were no signs. Did this mean no strangers ever came to town?

I rocked the boat and woke Papo as I came down from the bow, which interrupted my plan to slip by him and go ashore to explore. With a big smile he said, "I've arranged everything. We'll spend today in Para and we'll go with the other boats tomorrow."

I wondered what all he had arranged.

With my hood up, I followed Papo off the boat and into the market. The market amazed me. The fresh baked bread and cooking meats smelled so good. I would have eaten it without asking what it was. I watched a woman making a basket and a kid my age weaving cloth. Papo bought fresh bread, fruit and some cheese. I tore a hunk of bread off right there and started eating. I had not had supper in Altara last night, and no matter how much I eat at home, if I haven't eaten in Altara, I'm hungry in Altara. Papo, seeing me tear into the first loaf of bread, bought a second one. He also bought some cooked pies for our lunch. People greeted Papo, some called him Papo, and some called him Alrinar. People seemed curious about me, but I kept my head down, while at the same time, trying to see everything. I wanted to spend all day in the market, but Papo hurried me along.

One odd thing happened in the market. A woman bumped into me and to apologize, she bent down to look me in the face. When she stood up, I thought she and Papo exchanged glances. Papo acted like nothing happened.

After the market, we walked up into the town away from the river. I'm not sure whether to call Para a town or village. At the center of the town was the tallest and widest tree I have ever seen, tall and wide like an oak. A green surrounded the tree. At one end of the green, a spring flowed out of a large rock and filled a pool at the foot of the rock. People filled jugs with the water coming out of the rock, others washed clothes in the pool, some little kids played naked in the water. Papo and I refilled our water skins and continued our walk through the town.

Para occupies a peninsula surrounded by the Al. The majority of the town is near the docks where the boats are tied at the far end of the peninsula. The buildings grow less dense as the town moves away from the river. The houses on this side of town have large gardens and some small animals, mostly goats and chickens. They look like the goats and chickens you see at petting zoos.

The streets of Para are laid out in a grid pattern. To call them streets is an exaggeration. Only a few are wide enough to allow two carts to pass. Many are only wide enough for one cart. Some are so narrow, they are only paths between two buildings or two yards.

We left the town behind, climbing a ridge overlooking the whole peninsula. We spent the rest of the day there. We mostly just sat. At one point Papo finally began to elaborate on our plans. "Traditionally all the boats and people go from here to the next town, Nork, spend a day or two, then with all their boats and people joining us, we go to the next town. You and I will start out with the boats in the morning, stop at Nork and then go on to the site of the Gathering the next day, and leave the others behind."

If everything has a purpose, the purpose of this day and of his travel plans, were to keep me away from other people. I was being played like a pawn, but I was learning to think like a king. I asked, "So what is the Gathering?"

"Oh" Papo says, "Once a year the people from the five villages and the people who live scattered between the villages gather for a large market, games and ceremonies."

"Yat said this Gathering is special, because of the new Tara."

"Well yes, but the new Tara is just a boy." Papo turned away from me.

"Isn't the Tara your chief or leader?"

"We think of him as guide, at most the first among equals. He lives down the river and we don't have much need of him way up here."

"At some point he must have been something if he built a place like Lothar." I pointed out.

"The Tara who built Lothar died a long time ago. Remember I told you, the last true Tara built Lothar. Remember the story of the Taking. This Tara is descended from the brother of the true Tara, with each generation, the power of the Tara grows less and less. This new Tara will never be much of a Tara. He is not any older than you," he said, getting angry like he did the first time he mentioned the boy Tara up on the mountain. Afterwards he got quiet, as though he didn't mean to say everything he said.

We stayed up on the ridge until mid-afternoon. As we headed back into town we passed Yat and Evra. Papo barely acknowledged their existence. I gave them a slight wave. I wondered if they had been following us. On our morning walk, we went along the south side of the peninsula, we returned by the north side. By the time we reached the boats, only a few people were left in the market. Papo lead me back to our boat. However, today's journey gave me a good sense of the town. I could have found my way back to the boat on my own. I have been drawing a map in my mind. Our boat had been loaded with supplies.

Once on board, we settled down for the night. Papo prepared some supper. After we ate he insisted I take some sips from a small jug. He said it would help me sleep on the boat without getting seasick. I decided not to point out that I had no problem the previous night. I held my tongue over the mouth of the jug as I pretended to take a drink, even faking a swallow. The stuff had a foul odor.

I figured all this was because he wanted me to sleep, so I said goodnight and laid back and pretended to go to sleep. Less than a half an hour later, he slipped off the boat. I waited a few minutes, then followed. The moon had not yet risen, but like the night before, the stars were so many and so bright, I easily followed him from a distance. I stayed to the shadows as much as possible.

We crossed the open area where the market had been during the day. He went into a narrow path between two buildings. He turned a corner fifty feet in front of me. I moved quickly and quietly to the corner. Peering around the corner, he was nowhere in sight. The street was still and silent.

Farther down the street a light came out of one of the buildings and I thought I heard some voices. I moved down the street remaining in the shadows until I could see in the lighted building.

Papo sat at a table by the window with three other people, two men and a woman, the same woman who bumped into me in the market earlier in the day. He had arranged that bump so she could see my face. I slid up under the window to hear and not be seen. They were in the middle of a conversation.

A man spoke, "Don't we need to know where he comes from?"

Papo spoke, "I found him at Lothar, isn't that enough?"

They were talking about me.

The woman said, "I'm worried. There might be forces at work we don't understand. What do you say, Rosboes?"

The second man, I guess Rosboes, spoke, "There are no other forces. The boy is a gift, a gift for us."

Papo said, "Yes a gift, and at the Gathering, we share the gift with all of Altara."

The first man spoke challenging the plan, "What happens after we share the gift?"

Papo sounded frustrated, "If nothing else, there will be confusion and we demand the election of a new leader."

The first man spoke again, "A new leader, like Rosboes here."

Everyone said, "Yeah, yeah."

Rosboes asked, "What about your boy?"

Papo said, "When all is done, I'll take care of my boy and you take care of your boy."

I had heard enough. I didn't know the full plan, but clearly the plan did not end well for me or the other boy. I turned to leave only to come face to face with the guides Yat and Ra. Ra held his hand up as a sign to be quiet.

My mind went into hyper-drive trying to process what I had heard and my current situation. I asked myself,

What did Papo mean by 'take care of'?

Who is the other boy?

Did Yat and Ra follow me?

What did they know?

Are they friend or foe?

What if they are working with Papo?

I had three choices. Fight, but I didn't stand a chance against Yat and Ra, they were both twice my size. Talk, but would I know whether I was being told more lies. Or I could flee. I fled. I ran away from the boats, deeper into Para. They followed. After a few twists and turns I put a little distance between us and I hid to let them pass by me. (So much for their hunting skills.) I then worked my way around the town and back toward the boats. I occasionally disturbed the animals in people's gardens. People stuck their heads out the back door saying settle down and looking off into the darkness. When I was certain I had lost them I headed straight toward the boat. I threw off the hooded shirt. They had only seen me with the hood so now no disguise would be my disguise.

When I reached the area with the boats, all was quiet. A few people were on their boats, but no more than the previous night. I slowed down trying to move at a normal pace. However, I was breathing heavy and my heart was racing. I hadn't really thought about what I would do. I was just doing it.

I untied our boat at the post on the land and climbed aboard. There were poles in the boat and I used one to move the boat out into the river. I sank the pole into some mud right when the current grabbed the bow and turned the boat downstream. The mud held onto the pole and I let go of it. I floated down the center of the river. Para faded behind me and unknown places lay before me. My fate lay with the river Al. My body quit shaking. My breathing slowed. I felt physically safe, but my mind started asking,

Was there any way to keep from coming back to Altara?

If I was hurt here, would I really be hurt?

If I died here, would I be dead?

Where do I go next?

I had chosen to set off on my own without really thinking about what I would do next. I was so alone. I wished Fred was with me to tell me some stupid story. Why do I keep coming back to Altara? Nothing here has anything to do with me. I fell asleep determined to never return.

Chapter 8 Thursday Morning
King of Dweebs

I overslept this morning and rushed to get to the bus stop. I'm trying to figure out how to stop going to Altara. My night journeys originally felt like a game. They now feel like life. I thought about telling Mom what's been going on, but I'm not ready to do that. I used to dream about going to school in my pajamas and all day I walked around hoping nobody noticed. After last night in Altara, I would love to return to dreaming, even a pajama dream would be a welcomed relief.

At the bus stop, Fred pointed out I didn't have my math book, which meant I didn't have my homework. I headed back home at full speed. In the hallway outside my room, Larry decided to do a little, 'I'm going to block your way, move.' So I socked him in the shoulder and knocked him against the wall. As I came out of the house, the bus was coming down the street, so again I ran full out back to the bus stop.

The day got worse at school. I got off the bus and dropped all my books. I am such a klutz. Somewhere in picking my books up, my math homework got misplaced. So in math, I spent half the class searching for my homework. Two days ago, I was the cool guy playing chess with Coach and today, I turned back into super dweeb.

I need to find a way to stop going to Altara. I would rather be Henry the Dweeb alive in Suborediom than Henry the Dead of Altara. Maybe if I quit writing and worked on forgetting, it would go away. I don't have any friends there and Altara is not my life. This is my life. This is where I need to make friends. Here though, Fred and Jamal think they are something because some more people joined our table and because Coach said he would come back next Tuesday for a rematch. By lunch I calmed down, but I chose to go write instead of playing chess.

Telling this journal what I won't tell anyone else helps. The truth is I'm scared. I'm scared I'm a dweeb and I'm scared dweebdom is a black hole whose pull you can never escape. In Altara I am scared something bad will happen to me. I'm scared I might die.

And if all this wasn't enough, Jamal stopped me in the hall this afternoon and told me he and Fred decided at lunch, we need to go to the dance tomorrow night. And if that wasn't enough he convinced Gwen, Angela and Tanya to meet us there. (Tanya will be my date.) I am such a klutz and I have no idea what I'll say to her. This will prove for all time I not only dwell in dweebdom, but I am the king of dweebs.

I also haven't told anyone about my chin up bar. I go behind the garage and do chin ups every day. I did three yesterday. Failing to climb the rope will be one more proof I'm a dweeb.

When I got home my Mom started. "So you couldn't make it through a whole week without another incident. Could you?" (She's referring to the detention I got last week. I'll tell you about it some other time.)

She was talking about shoving Larry this morning. "I was in a hurry. I had forgotten my math homework and Larry wouldn't get out of the way. I was going to miss the bus." I thought this fully explained and justified my actions.

"So you hit him? Is hitting your solution for everything in life Henry? Are you going to go through life hitting whoever gets in your way?"

"I guess that won't work will it?" I knew she was right.

"Henry, what does your Dad say about fighting?"

"Dad says, 'boys fight, men talk."

"Then be a man Henry. Be a man."

"I will apologize to Larry and explain why his actions made me so mad. I understand punching him was not a solution and I'll work on using my words and not my fists." (I would rather just get punished.)

Tomorrow there's a science test and today Mrs. Ridley spent the day in review. I was so distracted, I didn't hear a word she said and I didn't take one single note. On the bus Fred promised to scan his notes and email them to me. He didn't send them till eight.

I finished studying science at ten. The test is about continental drift and rock types. I feel pretty good about all that. The test is at third period. I went to bed and tried to think about anything, but Altara, so I wouldn't go back. Then I thought I need to warn the other boy and fell asleep.

Chapter 9 Really Alone

I woke to a perfectly still boat. I thought I had been caught. Instead I discovered the boat had run aground on the left bank of the river, the grasslands side, but now there were woods. A rise of ground with bushes and trees separated me from the main channel. Judging by the sun, the morning was already half gone.

I climbed out of the boat and into about a foot of water. The boat floated free when I removed my weight.   I think that is the Archimedes Principle. I pulled the boat farther up the inlet and into some low hanging tree branches. I wanted the entire boat to be hidden from the main channel.

From the boat I retrieved food, water and another hooded shirt to replace the one I took off while fleeing last night. I've gotten comfortable wearing it, I think of it as my Altara uniform. Leaving the boat behind, I climbed up the embankment away from the river.

I sat down at the top of the riverbank looking into the woods and ate my breakfast. The food sat heavy on the knots that are my stomach.

I decided again to take stock of my situation. All the people I've met in this whole land are out to get me. The issue isn't anything I've done. They don't care where I came from or how I got here. My connection to Lothar is important. I'm a gift? I am a gift to benefit them, not to benefit me. Once they share Henry, the gift, I'm disposable. I am now at a location somewhere between the village of Para and the sea. The fact that this was forest and not grasslands meant I traveled some distance from Para. Possibly I floated past the location of the Gathering during the night, but I'm going to assume I didn't. Also I know Papo plans to travel by boat, so I plan to leave the boat behind. Oh and I need to find and warn the other boy. Warning the other boy is my mission.

In Alice in Wonderland, when Alice met the Cheshire cat, the cat sat in a tree above a divide in the road. Alice asked, "Which way should I go?" The Cheshire Cat asked, "Where do you want to get to?" Alice confessed she didn't know where she was going and the cat pointed out then it didn't matter which road she took. (I decided this was a rule.) So I needed a direction.

I started by finding the tallest tree on high ground. I considered TTV, Tree Top Viewing, the only available form of GPS and the next step toward choosing a direction. I am thinking like a king, but a king with very little Fire in his gut and no one to order around.

A small animal, about the size of a rabbit or squirrel, darted across the ground in front of me. I almost wet myself. What if it had been one of the cats from the grasslands? (I know if Fred or Jamal or any one reads this you're thinking 'What a wuss.' But let me ask if you have ever been alone? Have you ever had absolutely no idea where to find the nearest human being?)

I found a tree at the top of a rise. I exhausted myself jumping and failing to reach the lowest branch. I sat down at the base of the tree to rest, before going on.

Sometimes ideas come to me when I don't try so hard. I got up and found four rocks each about the size of my head. Two I carried over to a spot about two feet away from, right under the branch. The other two I had to roll into place. (In case you wondered, these appeared to be metamorphic rocks.) When I got them together, I stabilized them by putting sticks under them and by leaning them against each other. I had made a platform a foot high and eighteen inches square.

I stepped off twenty paces from my platform. I ran for it full out. On my final stride, I leapt to the platform and into the air to grab the branch. I actually held onto the branch. By walking my feet up the trunk of the tree and pulling up with my arms, I managed to get on top of the branch. I rested. The ground looked very far away. I easily climbed further up into the tree.   I was on a peninsula. The river on my right flowed to a point away from me then came back in my direction on my left. A village sat on the far bank opposite the point, this must be Nork or Tran, the next two villages that Papo mentioned. Turning around there were trees, more and more trees. My Mom once said to me 'you can't see the forest for the trees.' I think she meant the small and large pictures blend together. I studied the view. A good distance away, a shadow line ran through the trees. My eyes followed the line. It ran parallel to the river without taking all the twists and turns of the river. This must be a road and my next destination. I sat for a while at the top of the tree enjoying the freedom and the feeling of command I got from the overview of my surroundings. The Fire strengthened within me, until I noticed a lone boat coming down the river from Para. They were searching for me.

I needed to get down and I needed to get going. I didn't even hesitate as I dropped from the branch to the ground. Once on the ground, I headed toward the road.

Without a path, the going was slow and I kept thinking I should be at the road by now. I passed through a few clearings and they helped me check my directions. The day passed quickly, I estimated it was already early afternoon. I had not considered spending the night alone out here when I left the boat. I didn't even bring a sleeping mat. Now I doubted I could find my way back to the boat before dark or if I could find it at all.

But no, I will not change my plans. Man Rule Number Two is, "Even if the earth opens and swallows me alive, I will not change my plans." My Mom and Dad say that when we travel. Then they laugh about it.

If you are wondering, Man Rule Number One is, "No matter how many times I drive past the same gas station, I will not stop and ask directions." (I wanted a soda, a bag of Cheetos and some directions.)

I came on a clearing like the two or three others I had already passed through, but this time a movement on the other side caught my eye. I immediately crouched down. On the other side of the clearing, twenty yards away, stood a guy my size. He had his back to me. I didn't see anyone else.

This is rather embarrassing, but he was relieving himself, taking a whiz and well it's kind of rude to spy on someone taking a leak. (Henry Rule Number One: Don't spy on other guys while they take whizzes.) However, the fact that he was occupied gave me a chance to observe the situation and make a decision. I threw the hood up over my head and stepped quietly into the clearing. I walked about half the distance between us before he finished and turned around.

He was startled, but I was shocked. Quietly he said, "Well hello stranger."

I stood silent, frozen in place. I stared at him.

With a little laugh he spoke again, "Hey can you talk stranger?"

A Fire of confusion raged within me. On one hand I wanted to run, but on the other hand I wanted to tackle him full force. (I can't explain why I felt this way.) I didn't understand why he didn't get it. I heard my Dad saying, "Men talk, boys fight." If there was ever a time for me to be a man this was it. I had the hood on. I reached up and drew back the hood. I read every expression on his face, every twitch of his eye, and every part of his confusion. Now he was shocked. Please understand, we didn't just look alike, the similarity was shocking beyond belief. We were identical, our brown hair, our yet to develop muscles, everything. I stood facing myself.

My looks were the secret that made me a gift. This was the other boy.

He raised his left hand to show a small scar between his thumb and index finger. I raised my left hand and showed the same scar. I raised my right arm. I pointed to a mole near my elbow. He did the same. We stared at each other for a long time.

A voice calling from away in the woods broke our silence, "Are you ready?"

My other replied, "A little longer, I'll come when I'm done," and then he made a loud grunting noise as if taking a dump. We covered our mouths to silence our laughter.

He signaled for me to follow him. We moved away from the voice. He obviously did not want to be overheard.

"Who are you?" he asked speaking a little above a whisper.

"My name is Henry," I replied.

"Mine is Anree. Where are you from?"

"I'm not sure what to tell you except to say I am from very far away. Are you the Tara?"

"I will be when the people gather. Has anyone else seen you?"

"Only one person, an old guy, named Papo. Oh and a woman friend of his. Papo told me to always keep the hood up."

"Papo?" he said to himself obviously thinking. "Yes, Papo from Para, Alrinar is his real name."

"Yes, is he bad?" I asked.

"I'm sure he had a plan about how to use your 'natural good looks' to his advantage. I want to know more. Will you come with me?"

"Yes, I'll come." I wasn't going to stay in the woods by myself, and I was certain I came to Altara to find my identical other but why?

"Okay, one thing Alrinar was right about, is the fewer people who see your face," he then corrected himself, "our face, the better, at least until we figure out what is up. So put your hood up and keep your head down. Let me do the talking. We can be alone and talk when we get to my house."

I put my hood up and followed him across the clearing and a short way through the woods to the road I had seen from my perch in the tree. On the road a group of ten men on horseback waited for us.

Anree returning with me in tow obviously surprised them. He quickly took charge and spoke before they could ask. "Look what I found in the woods, my friend, Candor of Nork. We attended riding school together last summer. He's going to ride back with us."

The most in-charge-looking of the group, rode up to us, "Quite good he can ride behind me."

Anree replied, "Now, Rosboes, your poor horse complains of carrying you, my horse will be glad to carry the two of us. Anree mounted his horse and reached down to help me. In a rather clumsy move, I managed to climb up behind him. We rode off in silence, heading east, the same direction as the flow of the river.

I didn't want to ride with that guy, so I appreciated Anree speaking up. I whispered, "Who is that guy?"

"He's Rosboes, my guardian," Anree replied.

"Was he in Para last night?" I asked, trying to keep my voice calm and neutral.

"Yes, in fact we are out on the road because we came to meet him on his way back to Roan. It was an excuse to get out and go riding for the day. I didn't care if he came back or not. At the

Gathering, I will be the Tara in my own right and I will no longer have a guardian. We need to be quiet now. We will talk tonight when we can't be overheard."

Yes, I thought, tonight we will talk. I am certain I am here to save Anree from Papo's plot.

As we rode I thought about Fred and Jamal's plan for the dance. I tried to make a list in my mind of things to talk to Tanya about. I thought I should let her talk and I planned to ask her about movies she's seen or music or what she reads. I will ask her why she likes that music or that type of book. I know this is going to be so lame. I am the king of dweebs. My stomach was just one solid knot.

Rosboes came up beside us interrupting my thoughts, "Candor, what were you doing alone in the forest?"

Even before I realized he meant me, Anree jumped in with, "Oh my friend is tired and he does not want to admit he lost his way so close to his home. But tell me Rosboes, was your trip to Para productive?"

"Oh yes quite productive," he replied with a smile.

"And will many be coming to the Gathering," Anree asked.

"Oh I believe everyone up and down the river will be at the Gathering," he replied still with a smile.

"And what of that old man, the friend of yours, what's his name, yes, Alrinar? Did you see Alrinar in Para?" Anree asked. Anree already knew everything I wanted to tell him before I had told him anything. And he used what I hadn't even told him to test or maybe trap Rosboes.

"Ah, old Alrinar, I haven't seen him in a long while," Rosboes slowed his horse to let us go ahead.

I whispered, "He lied. They were together last night."

Anree replied, "Yes he lied. We must wait and talk tonight."

I am not sure how long or how far we rode, but by the time we reach Roan, I was sore and tired. Roan is the main city of Altara and home of the Tara. Even on first impressions, Roan was clearly much larger than Para.

No trumpets or fanfare announced our arrival. As we passed through town, Anree called out to people and people called out to him. Riding with Anree was more like being a member of the basketball team than the chess team.

Anree's house stood at the center of town. The house reminded me of Lothar, but larger and definitely not in ruins. We rode through gates into a large central courtyard where we all dismounted. A tree like the one on the green in Para filled the center of the courtyard. One of the men took our horse and everyone seemed to disperse in different directions. Rosboes seemed ready to tell Anree something, but Anree spoke first.

"Candor and I are going up to my rooms. Please have the kitchen send up supper," he said speaking politely, but also firmly. He started to turn away then turned back saying, "Did you want to ask me something?"

"No, no I can wait," Rosboes replied.

I followed Anree across the courtyard and upstairs to a third floor set of four rooms. The rest of the house had only two stories so these rooms stood above the rest of the house with views in all four directions.

Tossing his stuff on the floor, he said, "I live here alone now. When I was younger, like six months ago, my Memere (His Grandmother) lived in that room," pointing to one of the side rooms.

A guy definitely lived here. They were great rooms. He threw himself down on some floor pillows and I followed suit landing nearby.

"Okay, tell me where you are from and who you are," he said.

"Like I said, my name is Henry and I come from a place very different from here." I didn't say anything to Anree, but when I said my name aloud I heard, for the first time, the similarity between Anree and Henry. Maybe he heard it also.

I continued my story. "We have cars and bicycles, and paved roads, and I go to school."

I thought all this must be confusing for him, but he kept nodding his head, and said, "I can picture everything you say, but it is a lot to take in and like you said your home must be far from here. So now tell me how you came here."

So I started with the horse and the ride. He made me carefully describe the horse. I told him about Papo and the guides. He said Papo probably started plotting when he met me, but he thought the guides might have been trying to protect me. He also assured me no one in Altara sold orphan boys into slavery. He started to get mad, when I told him what I overheard between Papo and

Rosboes, especially 'You take care of your boy and I'll take care of my boy.' He gets mad like I do, but he quickly calms down.

He filled me in on parts of the story. From the tree I had seen Nork, and yes, Candor is a real person. I told the story of the Taking. He knew the story, but he thought his Memere told it differently.

When I finished, he told me his story. Yes, his great-great-grandfather had been the brother of the last true Tara. And at the Gathering, at the fullness of thirteen years, he would continue the line of the not-quite-true Tara.

The people of Altara have always thought there were other peoples, but they have never found them. Exploring groups have traveled as much as a month in every direction without meeting anyone. So his father had a boat made twice the size of the riverboats and with sails. His father planned a long voyage along the coast. As a test, his mother and father set off with a crew on a three or four-day trip. They were never seen again. Three years have passed. Memere has cared for him and Rosboes, acting as guardian, has run Altara as he pleased. This made Anree sad, so he wanted me to tell him about my family and my friends.

I told him about Fred and Jamal. Then he said, "Isn't there a dance?" I told him about the girls and Tanya. I told him about my Mom and Dad, but he especially wanted to know about Larry. He liked the idea of a little brother. (I also prefer the idea over the real thing.) And for each of us, as the other talked, we remembered and knew more than we were told.

Someone brought dinner to us. I hid when they came in the room. We talked through dinner and into the night until we fell asleep.

Chapter 10 Friday at School
The Dance

Mom started talking about the dance at breakfast this morning, saying I shouldn't be scared. I guess Jamal put something on Facebook last night. As I headed for the bus, I realized, I live in two separate worlds, both of which are trying to destroy me.

I did fine on the science test at third period.

The girls joined us for lunch. Supposedly, Jamal challenged Angela to a chess match. They were as interested in chess as I am in turtles. Really Jamal cooked up the whole dance plan as a way to go with Angela and they cooked up the chess match to get Fred and me to the table with Gwen and Tanya. The end of lunch came as a huge relief

I like Tanya. I think she is cute, but she's at least three inches taller than me so I don't know how that will affect dancing. I worry the whole time I am with her that I will embarrass myself. My first attempts at conversation were, as I expected, lame. I finally gave up and tried to flash her Anree's smile every so often. She smiled back. I hope tonight goes better. (Have I told you Anree has a great smile? I practiced smiling like Anree in front of the mirror this morning.)

Today in gym class, all the jock guys climbed the rope. I tried to study their techniques. They use their legs to hold their position on the rope then reach higher with their hands. I hate that rope. The whole afternoon at school blurred together. My mind struggled to decide whether to worry about what is happening in Altara or to worry about what to wear to the dance tonight, while at the same time trying to figure out how to climb the rope.

I struggle with what to wear right up until the last minute. Finally Mom came into my room and we agreed on a clean pair of jeans and a blue polo shirt. She preferred a red one, but I feared I would stand out too much. Every time I turned around, Larry made fun of the way I combed my hair or did anything. I wanted to punch him, but instead I locked him out of my room. When he howled, "Henry is in love." Dad finally made him behave. My Dad insisted on taking my picture before I left. I can't imagine wanting to remember this night. Fred's dads are driving us to the dance and Jamal's parents will pick us up.

Gwen, Angela and Tanya all came together and arrived when we did. Jamal and Angela both have phones and had been texting back and forth to make this happen. I hoped we look more like a group and less like three couples.

Music was playing when we walked into the gym. The strobe lights and a disco ball distracted little from the gymness of the room. The theme of the decorations was 'Tropical Survivor'. They decorated the rope with paper leaves to look like a vine. (I did five chin ups this afternoon. I hate that rope.)

Mr. Michaels, the band teacher, played the music. He put together a playlist from suggestions kids gave him throughout the week. Every time a new song started, I said to myself, 'Thank goodness it's not a slow one.' For the first thirty minutes, everyone stood around being awkward. Finally Coach and Mrs. Ridley led off dancing and we joined in. I was actually coordinated. After a few dances Tanya and I headed to the concession stand for nachos and soda. Fred came up behind me saying he had no money. Fortunately my Mom gave me money and I had enough to help Fred out.

Tanya and I found a table and sat down. Fred, Gwen, Jamal and Angela came over to join us. Jamal and Angela couldn't have sat any closer if they sat on the same chair.

The conversation paused and Fred got nervous. His mouth started running faster than his brain. First he talked about Coach and Mrs. Ridley and he wondered if Mr. Ridley knew about them dancing. He then claimed one of the football players had a flask of liquor and he would spike your drink for a dollar. Fred had not seen the flask nor did he know the player's name, but he swore to the truth of the story.

I wanted to shut him down before he found a new subject, so I said, "I'll give you a quarter for each slice of jalapeño you can eat without taking a drink."

Fred jumped on my offer. "Get your money out because I'm going to take it all."

Jamal came up out of their cocoon to say, "I think he needs to wait fifteen seconds between each jalapeno."

Jamal is always ready to create rules for a game, even where none are needed. He also has a watch that does twenty-five different things. His watch can tell you the time in three different time zones, be an alarm clock and serve as a stopwatch. Jamal would also want me to mention it can accurately perform all these tasks from one hundred feet underwater or up into stratosphere. So Jamal decided to time fifteen seconds between each jalapeño. A small crowd gathered for the game.

Jane from science class said, "Fred, don't do it. It's just a silly bet." A few of the other girls joined in with cautions about getting sick and burning holes in his stomach. All the guys said go for it.

So Fred, with a smile on his face, ate the first one, commenting, "Delightful."

Jamal with the stopwatch counted, "... eleven, twelve, thirteen, fourteen, fifteen."

Still with a smile, Fred ate the second one. With less confidence he said, "Better than the first."

Jamal counted in Spanish, "... once, doce, trece, catorce, quince."

Fred started looking through the tray as if searching for just the right jalapeño.

"Quit stalling," Tervel called out.

Fred popped the third one into his mouth. Even in the dim light his face was visibly red.

Jamal counted in French, "...onze, douze, treize, quatorze, quinze."

Gwen grabbed Fred's arm and said, "Don't be silly, Fred, stop this right now."

Jamal, trying to sound like an official announcer said, "Does the contestant wish to continue?"

Fred went for the fourth one. He swallowed without even chewing. He began to perspire.

Jamal counted in Esperanto, " … ok, nau, dek, dek unu, dek du, dek tri, dek kvar …", but before he got to fifteen, Angela, in a surprise move, grabbed the tray with the remaining jalapeños, marched over to the trash can and dumped them in. All the girls applauded and they followed her to the other side of the gym.

As soon as Fred finished chugging down his soda, he held out his hand to me saying, "Where's my dollar?"

Rather than point out I had given him five dollars earlier, I gave him a dollar. Fred, Jamal, Tervel, Dante and some other guys started to replay the whole great jalapeño contest. As I moved away, Fred boasted, "If the concession stand wasn't closed, I would eat four more."

I guess I was more interested in Tanya than I thought. In chess and in life, I have been thinking more about my strategies. If the purpose of the dance was to be with the girls, then we sabotaged our own mission. No, I sabotaged my mission.

I moved slowly around the edge of the gym and came up behind Tanya. I tapped her on the shoulder, gave her Anree's smile and motioned for her to step back from the group.

"I'm sorry for starting that ruckus. I wanted to quiet Fred down."

"You wanted to quiet him down by setting him on fire?"

"Obviously I didn't think things through."

"It was a little funny," she said with a smile.

Mr. Michael's voice came on the speakers interrupting our reconciliation, "This is the last dance of the night, this one is the slow one we've all been waiting for, so don't be shy."

Tanya and I and two dozen other couples took to the dance floor as the evening ended. Coach and Mrs. Ridley were one of the other couples. I was Henry on Fire in Suborediom.

Now sleep. Now Altara.

Chapter 11 Boys' Day Out

The morning sun poured through Anree's windows filling the room. I awoke in Altara with thoughts of my life at home. I had been to my first dance. I danced with a girl and survived. In fact I have been on my first date.

Anree was already awake and washing at a water bowl. He rummaged around in trunks looking for clothes while I washed. He kept pestering me for details about the dance. I told him I survived, but I more than survived.

Finally he let up on the dance and announced "We are out of here today. We'll go someplace where we can think and talk. I've got clothes we can wear to help us blend in until we get out of town."

Someone knocked at the door. Anree motioned for me to step out of sight as he opened the door.

A woman's voice said, "Here's your breakfast."

"Thanks, Mora," Anree replied.

"Oh and Rosboes wants you and your friend to join him for lunch."

"Oh Mora, he is so thoughtful." The tone of his voice told me Mora understood how unappealing an invitation this was. "But my friend is a bit under the weather after his ordeal and we will be staying in my rooms all day. In fact, when you bring our lunch, we won't need it. Please tell Rosboes how sorry we are."

The door shut and Anree turned and smiled at me as I stepped back into the room, "Rosboes wants to get a look at you."

71

"Well I don't want another look at him. What did you mean when you said we won't need our lunch?" I asked, thinking I will probably want my lunch.

"Oh, that's my way of telling Mora we are going out and she is welcome to come up here and eat lunch. This way, if any one questions her about where I've gone, she doesn't have to lie. I think she has a boyfriend she brings but I'm not sure who he is. Anyway put these on and let's get out of here," he said throwing me some clothes.

Anree had assembled two outfits. Of course everything fit me. The clothes were a bit drab and not as refined as the clothes he wore yesterday. As we dressed he said, "We'll add a little dirt getting out of here and not even your mother would know us."

This mention of my Mom struck me as odd and stirred the Fire in me. I followed him out the window and across the roof of the house. All I could think of was the time my Dad slid off the roof. We easily climbed down an outside wall.

Once on the ground, we put on hats to hide our faces. He led us along the side of the house to a place where the parts of the building joined creating a hiding place. In the corner, Mora had left two bags and two walking sticks for us.

"Mora thinks of everything. Don't worry about getting back in, she'll leave a door unlocked for us." The bags had shoulder straps to go across our chests. We put the bags on, checked to make sure no one was watching, and stepped out into the town.

I was glad to get out of the house and visit the town. Like I said before, Roan is bigger than Para and more of a city. Unfortunately Anree, like Papo, was focused on me not being seen and hurried us through town. We kept our heads down and, when someone was in our way, we stepped aside.

Roan sits on a bluff and a large flood plain, at least a mile wide, separates it from the river. A road leads from Roan across the plain to docks on the river. We followed the road briefly, then turned upriver across the plain. We were going to Anree's favorite fishing spot.

We walked at least a couple of miles. Anree seemed content to walk in silence and I enjoyed the morning. We looked like a couple of guys without a care in the world. We crossed another road as we neared the river.

"This is the river road," Anree explained. "It runs from Rahtol at the sea past Roan and Altara to ford the Al at Tran and then continues up the other side of the river to Nork and Para. But most people travel by boat."

"I understand coming down stream by boat, but isn't going upstream hard work?"

"Actually the wind almost always blows from the sea up the river so we can use sails to move upstream."

"And what do you mean by saying the road passes Altara? I thought the whole valley was Altara." I was confused.

"The land is Altara but we also call the place of the Gathering Altara. I can't wait to show it to you."

I still think it's confusing.

After we crossed the road, we climbed over some rocks to get to the river. There was a beach and also a rock ledge that jutted out over the river about ten feet above the water.

We sat down on the ledge. Anree showed me that the end of each walking stick actually had been split. Anree pulled from his belt a leather pouch with bone spear points. We slid the shaft of the point into the split in the wood and wrapped it tight with a leather string. I had to redo mine twice to get it tight enough to hold the point in place.

"Where I come from we have a river called the Mississippi," I said.

"Miss-a-sip-ee," Anree sounded the word out slowly.

"Yes, and there are stories about Tom Sawyer and Huck Finn who live along the river. The stories are about how they get in and out of trouble, but all they want to do is spend their day fishing," I explained.

"If I went home with you, could I meet them?" he asked sincerely.

"No, they are characters in a story, and I don't think you can go home with me." I said. I was embarrassed that I confused him but I also didn't like the idea of him going home with me.

"Maybe I could meet Fred and Jamal or even Tanya?"

"I don't think anything like that is going to happen." I turned red.

"Maybe someday," he said.

We took our spears and waded into the water. Anree motioned for me to stand still and to be quiet. Within minutes, several fish swam near us.

Anree motioned for us both to strike. We did. Anree brought his spear up with a fish. I came up with nothing.

Anree laughed at me, "I forgot to tell you the fish is not where you see it. The water plays a trick on you. You strike a little beyond the fish."

I should have known this. It's called refraction. I know the word. He knows the meaning. We started over, standing still. This time when we struck, we both came up with a fish. I caught my first fish. I wanted Anree to take it off the spear for me. He refused. So I took it off myself and went back to catch another. We cleaned them and started a fire on the beach to cook them for lunch.

While we waited for the fire to build up, I wanted to get to the matter at hand. I said, "What do Papo and Rosboes hope to accomplish by popping up at the Gathering with an extra you."

"Well I'm not sure, but they could cause a lot of confusion." After a little silence he went on, "I think Rosboes wants to be the new Tara, but I think the others want each town to be independent and maybe the head of each town take a turn being the Tara."

"Honestly that doesn't sound all bad to me," I said.

"No, the idea is not bad, in and of itself, but I think their motives are wrong."

"How so?" I asked.

"The Tara protects the average person from the rich and powerful of their own village.

75

Without my father, most of the land in Para would be in the hands of two or three people. My father always told me the strength of the Tara is built not on wealth or arms, but on the love of the people. He told me, I would be no greater than my love for the people."

"Wow, what a great view of government. Does it work?"

"If we had a true Tara, it would work better," he said with sadness in his voice.

"Now, after all these years, what keeps you from being the true Tara."

"My Father said it would never be so, but I think I need the symbols of the true Tara. I need to get back what was lost. I need to open the gates of Altara and I need the unicorn to be seen in the land." He sounded hopeless.

"So you believe the unicorn took the boy and the key and left?"

"Yes."

"So the unicorn is a problem, but can't we just make a new key? What does it look like?"

"I've never seen the key but the keyhole is something like this." He drew in the sand what looked like a double skeleton key hole, a key where teeth go both up and down from a center shaft. "They've tried a couple of times to make a key but never succeeded."

"The keyhole reminds me of something, but I don't know what," I said thinking out loud.

The fire had burned to coals and I went to add more sticks, but Anree stopped me. He wrapped each fish in large wet leaves, laid them on the coals and covered the fire with dirt.

"Now a swim," he said and started taking off his clothes. He ran up onto the rock ledge and leapt in to the river cannonball style.

I took off my clothes and followed at a more cautious pace, but I was not going to be chicken in front of Anree. I ran, jumped and gravity did the rest. The day had gotten warm and the cool river water felt good.

We got out at the beach near our fire. I put my pants on as soon as I got out. Anree laid on the rock to dry in the sun. (If you are wondering, and I don't need any snickering from Fred and Jamal, I can confirm we are identical.)

Anree dressed after a while and we had our fish. Mora had also put bread and fruit in our bags. The fruit was sweet like a peach or an apricot. After lunch we laid on the rock. What a great day.

Not meaning to speak out loud I said, "I wonder why the unicorn left."

Anree rolled over and looked at me, "Now you're asking the right question. Memere says there are no unicorns. In fact, sometimes when she tells the story of the Taking, she says a horse took the boy away."

"You know people don't always tell the whole story if something bad or embarrassing happened."

"Back at Roan, we'll ask Memere to tell us the story of the taking."

"Won't two grandsons upset her?" I asked. I wondered how my grandmother would react.

"She doesn't see so well, I think we will be okay," he said.

Before we left, we speared some fish to take back to Mora. We put back on what I now think of as our Tom and Huck outfits. We put out the fire and headed home.

As we came over the rocks to the road, three people on horseback were on the road headed toward Roan. We ducked out of sight until they passed by, then we spied on them from behind.

"The one on the left is definitely Papo," I said.

"The others are Hara from Nork and Bar from Tran. Rosboes is gathering a council. He is going to make his move before we go to Altara for the Gathering," he said smiling.

"Aren't you worried?" I asked.

"A little, but my father trained me for this and Memere would tell me stories of my Father to help me remember the things he had tried to teach me. My father said always be honest with the people. We will need to tell the people about the two Taras before they do."

"Two Taras? I don't think so. There is one Anree, the Tara, and one Henry, who belongs somewhere else." We were walking by now.

"I don't think that way," he said with an annoying confidence. "We share looks, rather good looks, I think. (He thinks he is so funny every time he refers to our good looks.) And we share memories. Yes, there are two Anrees and two Henrys."

"Are you hatching a plot?" I asked.

Repeating my words and laughing he said, "Are you hatching a plot? Sometimes we say the oddest things."

I shouted at him, "I said 'hatching a plot.' Anree said some stupid thing about two Anrees and two Henrys."

"I, we, they are such little words." he said laughing at my discomfort and anger. I was stirred up. I wanted to jump him from behind and make him understand there was one Henry sitting on top of him and one Anree pinned to the ground. I don't know why. I felt he was taking something from me with his two Henrys. He was taking something I didn't want to give. Finally I gave in. I dropped my stuff and jumped him from behind. In my head, as I took him to the ground I heard my Dad saying, "Boys fight, men talk," but today, I was the boy Henry.

Unfortunately, once again, I had not thought through my actions. On my surprise move, I downed Anree, but once the surprise passed, we were evenly matched. So he flipped over and threw me off. We rolled over a couple of times wrestling, no punches. We finally stopped and started laughing at ourselves.

"That was fun," Anree said. We walked in silence and I began to calm down. I didn't want to talk, but I kept thinking about two Taras and two Henrys. What would Altara do with two Taras? What would my Mom do with two Henrys?

Back at Roan, we realized there was a problem getting two Anrees back into the house.

"I guess two of us going in through the kitchen won't work," I said.

"Not yet, at least."

I half frowned, half smiled. I was still trying to wrap my mind around how two Anrees or two

Henrys would work anywhere. "I guess we will just have to climb back up the outside wall."

We returned our sacks and sticks to where we found them. We also left the fish for Mora. We went to climb up the building at the same spot where we climbed down. Our climb back in was easier than I expected. Instead of returning to the roof, we climbed in a window on the second floor. We slipped through the hallway as if heading to our rooms, but then Anree turned down a different hallway. I tried to ask what was up, but he told me to be quiet. We paused and knocked at a door. A small voice on the other side said, "Come in."

When Anree stepped into the room, a whole new energy came over him. A small woman sat in a chair by a small fire. Anree gave her a big hug and stepped back.

"Memere," he said, "This is Henry."

"Mora told me you had a guest, but she said he was your friend Candor from Nork. Maybe you are up to something Anree?" she said grinning.

She didn't see so well, but she didn't miss much.

"Yes, Memere, we are up to something, but his real name is Henry and I want you to meet him."

"Anree, you're grown up now. You don't need to tell me all your secrets." Turning toward me she said, "Henry, come closer, I don't see very well."

I stepped closer. She pulled me down and squinted at my face. Her right hand came up to touch my left cheek.

In her small voice she whispered, "You are a good looking boy. You are good looking like my Anree."

"Thank you," I stammered.

"Memere, tell us the story of the night of the Taking, tell us the true story. Tell us why the unicorn left." We sat down by her feet.

She seemed to drift a little. "The unicorn can never come back. The unicorn was taken from us."

The Fire in me leapt at her words. I couldn't help myself. I jumped in with, "How?"

Though we occasionally interrupted her, this is the story of the night of the Taking as told to us by our Memere.

The season at Lothar had come to the end. On the last day, the people gathered for a celebration. As the sun set, the Tara called his son to the center of the gathering. The boy was no older than the two of you.

The Tara proclaimed, "This is my son, the heir of my Tara. With this key to the gates of Altara, I declare him our future leader." And he took the key on a leather strap and hung it around Anree's neck. She smiled at Anree saying, "You are named for him." (I am pretty sure Anree already knew this.)

The people cheered and they carried Anree and the Tara around on their shoulders for an hour. Then things began to settle down for the night. The sky was dark and rain was coming. The Tara and his family headed up to Lothar. Most of the people retired to their sleeping area.

The celebration continued in the camp of the hunters late into the night. They had three, maybe four bonfires burning. From nowhere, the unicorn leapt into the center of the gathering. The hunters jumped to their feet. Out of their instinct to hunt, they began to form a circle around the creature. They held burning sticks in the air. Then someone shouted, "Give me rope." Another shouted, "Tighten the circle." They were daring to hunt what no one had ever dared to hunt.

They threw ropes over his neck. The animal reared up on his hind legs. They threw a rope around its front feet and brought down the creature. They pinned him to the ground. The animal fought them, with a saw they cut the horn from the unicorn. The creature cried out with a sound that pierced the soul of the mountain.

They say Rosboes' great-grandfather took the horn and held it high as a sign of victory. As he held the horn up in the air, thunder shook the foundations of the mountain and the skies opened with torrents of rain. The people scattered to their rooms and tents. The unicorn broke free and galloped up the mountain toward the house. For an hour, the rain came down so hard you could barely see. Then as suddenly as it began it ended. The sky cleared. The moon came out.

The people began to sleep until a cry came from the house, "The boy is missing." Every hunter and tracker was given a part of the mountain to search and then they searched again, but they found no trace of the boy or the unicorn. For the next twelve days, they searched the mountain. The Tara ordered the buildings torn apart to search for a hiding place. The unicorn and the boy were gone.

Memere was almost crying as she finished the story. We held her hand and comforted her. Before we left she said, "We, all of Altara, has suffered for all these years for what those people did. How can anyone ever make right something that was so wrong?"

We walked back to our rooms in silence. Once in our rooms, we had a lot to talk about.

"So when Papo told the story, the boy was taken, but in this story the horn of the unicorn was taken and the boy is missing." I said.

Anree said, "And if you take the horn from a unicorn, it's a horse or a hornless unicorn. I think if the Tara is to be a true Tara, we must right this wrong. We need to find the horn they took from the unicorn."

"We only have unicorns in stories, but I have never heard of anything as brutal as cutting the horn from a unicorn. Do you think the horn still exists?" I asked.

"It must be somewhere," he said.

I guess I understood why the unicorn left Altara, and right before I fell asleep, I realized the horse that brought me here was the hornless unicorn. I have ridden the unicorn. The unicorn has returned.

Chapter 12 Saturday at Home
A Second Date

I began to warm to the idea of two Henrys. I wished there were two Henrys today. I would let the other Henry mow the yard and wash the car. I washed the car to pay back the money Mom gave me for the dance last night. As usual, all Larry did today was clean his room.

I kept telling Anree there is nothing great about having a little brother. He says I only think that because I have one. I told him if I could give him Larry, I would. After mowing the yard, I did seven chin-ups. I am growing stronger. Dad had been in a bad mood when he came home from work yesterday but he came out and helped me wash the car and we even had a bit of a water fight. I finished my chores by noon.

At one, I called Jamal for a conference call with him and Fred. Fred jumped right in, "If those girls hadn't shut me down, I could have done another four or five jalapenos."

I was back at him, "First off, that's not true and second, it was a dance, not a jalapeno eating contest. We were there to be with the girls and apparently girls don't like jalapeno eating contests."

Jamal said, "You are so right, Henry, and Fred, if you don't learn to be cooler, I am going to leave you out of future plans." (Like he was in charge of our social calendar? I guess though we wouldn't have gone to the dance if he had not set it up.)

"So Jamal, you and Angela seemed to be getting close," I said this mostly to tease him about the way they were all over each other, but he didn't hear the tease in my voice.

"Yes, we almost kissed," he said back quite sincerely.

Fred couldn't contain himself, he almost shouted, "What is an almost kiss?"

Jamal trying to sound mature said, "When you care more about girls than eating jalapenos, you might find out. Anyway you two hang loose, I am working on us meeting the girls at the mall at four. We can leave about 3:30 on our bikes. I'll email you around three to confirm." As we all hung up, I realized Jamal was in charge of our social calendar, at least for now.

At three thirty, we left for the mall on our bikes. The mall is fifteen or, at the most, twenty minutes away by bike, but Jamal kept calling out, "Slow down."

"Why," Fred, who was in the lead, shouted.

"Slow down or you'll sweat," Jamal shouted back.

"What?" Fred shouted hitting his brakes. We all stopped.

"You'll sweat." Jamal said.

Fred sniffed under his arms, "And the point is what?"

"Girls don't like sweaty or smelly boys," Jamal said with an emphasis on smelly. Jamal took the lead riding at a leisurely pace.

As we pedaled along, Fred kept sniffing under his arms. I wasn't sure whether he was making fun of Jamal or was worried he might be a smelly boy.

85

(I think this rates being a Henry rule. Smelly boys are not lucky boys.) When we got to the mall, we locked up our bikes. Jamal insisted we go into the men's room and 'freshen up' which meant splashing some water on our faces and combing our hair with our fingers. Jamal also had some breath mints. We met the girls in the food court.

We soon separated into couples. It seemed to have been a plan on the part of the girls. We were all sitting at a table in the food court when Angela said, "Jamal, come see these earrings I've been thinking about buying." And they were gone.

Then Gwen said, "Fred will you teach me how to play Guitar Hero in the arcade." And they were gone.

"I had a nice time at the dance last night," Tanya said.

"I did too," I said. "I was scared about going, you know, about dancing and stuff."

"Me too, but I had a good time. And you're a good dancer and what about Mrs. Ridley and Coach?"

And so we talked for about an hour. We talked about everything, that is, except Altara. I still haven't told anyone about Altara. I'm afraid they will think I'm crazy. Or maybe I'm afraid if I tell, Altara will go away. I tell Anree about everything that happens here and this doesn't go away.

We left the mall at five thirty to make sure we were home before dark. I'm not sure what's happening, I can't stop thinking about Tanya. I wonder if she is thinking about me. I'm actually looking forward to Monday when I'll see her again.

I set my alarm, because I agreed to go to Church with Fred in the morning. Now I'm off to sleep and Altara.

Chapter 13 The First Reveal

Mora came knocking about thirty minutes after we woke. I stepped into one of the other rooms as she brought in breakfast.

"So how are Rosboes' guests?" Anree asked.

"No one cares for them. They treat everyone, oh I don't know the word, but they don't respect any of us," she said sounding a bit mad.

"Do you think they respect me?"

"Oh that's the worst, not at all. Last night they were asking all kinds of questions about you and your friend. Saying 'what have the boys been up to.' And Hara from Nork says she saw Candor in Nork yesterday, so your friend can't be Candor. They want to know who he is," her voice was shaking. She was getting quite upset, but before Anree spoke she started again, "And why did you and your friend make your grandmother tell you that story last night. She worried all night long."

"Everything is okay. I didn't mean to upset Memere."

"Having her tell you that old story is what did it. Why would you care about all that old stuff from before we were born?"

"Tell Memere, tell everyone in the house all is okay. Before the week is over I will be the Tara and all will be right." Even I felt reassured by his confidence.

"Oh I wish I believed you. You are so young and they don't want you to be the Tara."

"Mora, I need you to believe in me. I need you to tell people with certainty everything is good. The people of this house trust you." As he talked,

88

neither of us imagined what he planned to do next, especially not Mora. He called to me saying, "Anree, will you come out here please."

I hesitated. He called again. Mora was looking at Anree as I stepped into the room, noticing my movement, she turned to see me. All the color faded from her face. She opened her mouth as if she is going to scream, but she was silent and fell to her knees uttering, "May the wind be with me and the river Al give me strength."

The Fire in me was strong. I went over and gently took her hand. "Mora, get up. It's good. It's okay. In four days there will be a true Tara."

Anree spoke, "You must tell people the Tara will not fail them. The land will remain at peace and justice will be abundant."

"Now, later today, Rosboes will send for my friend, 'Candor,' and me," I said.

Anree took up, saying, "If we are not here when you come to tell us, go back and tell him we will meet with his council tomorrow morning. Will you do that?"

She nodded.

I continued, "Do you understand I'm not a boy anymore. I'm ready to be the Tara. Do you believe me? Do you believe us?"

"I believe, though I do not understand," she said going out of the room.

Revealing ourselves to Mora started a course of events we would not be able to stop.

Half thinking aloud and half talking to me, he said, "Rosboes is sure to be using the room where he and Father used to meet. We can listen and even watch from the room above."

"Will we be safe?" I asked.

"I don't think anything will be truly safe from here on out," he said with a tremble that made me shiver. I wondered if his confidence was all a show for Mora.

I followed him through a labyrinth of hallways on the second floor of the house. We fortunately passed no one. Our journey ended in a small windowless room with an inside opening to a large two story room on the first floor. We peeped over the ledge. Papo and Rosboes sat at either end of a table. We dropped back down and Anree whispered to me, "The amazing thing is we can clearly hear them and as long as we whisper, they can't hear us."

Hara of Nork and Bar of Tran came in. They all greeted each other before they settled down to business.

"Why is no one here from Rahtol, Roan or Altara?" I asked.

"No one lives at Altara except during the week of the Gathering and Rosboes thinks he speaks for both Rahtol and Roan."

Papo retold his story of finding me up at Lothar.

Hara said, "I am troubled that we don't know where he came from."

Papo said, "He came from Lothar. Isn't that enough?"

Rosboes sounding impatient said, "Papo always thought he would return."

"People also expect the unicorn to return," Hara said.

"The unicorn is a myth, a story," Rosboes said.

"Myths, such as the rule of the Tara?" Bar said.

"Yes, stories of the past told to amuse children," Rosboes said.

"So what is your plan?" Hara asked.

Rosboes told them, "We remain silent about the two of them until the ceremony. We keep track of his shadow friend 'Candor' and at the ceremony we pull the hood off 'Candor."

"And then what?" Bar asked.

"We went through all this in Para. Confusion will follow and I am certain we can convince the people two Taras are the same as no Taras." Rosboes believed everyone should see the pure genius of his plan by now.

However Hara was also skeptical saying, "Two Taras might be twice as much Tara to deal with. More is usually more."

Rosboes said, "I tell you two Taras are as good as no Taras. Papo you are quiet. What do you think?"

Papo, who seemed to play the elder in this council, said, "I think it could go either way. I think the important thing is what we offer in place of the Tara."

"Yes, what we offer," Rosboes went on. "We will tell each town they can choose their own leaders and decide their own ways. No longer will people need to wait until the Gathering or come to Roan to the Tara to claim their justice. The people will like the sound of it very much."

Papo spoke next, "What about the boys?"

"They can follow the parents on a one way trip out to sea." Rosboes tone made clear he meant to be rid of us.

91

We had heard enough, Anree gave me a signal to follow him and he lead us back to our rooms.

Our lunch was waiting when we arrived. A short while later Mora knocked on the door. I called out, "Come in."

Looking from one to the other of us as she talked, Mora said, "They asked for the 'Tara to be' to come down to meet with them."

I asked, "Anree what do you think?"

"I lean toward waiting until tomorrow. What do you think?" he said.

"I like to know what my opponent is thinking, and the sooner the better." (I think this is a Henry rule. Maybe number 4. When Jamal gets a new book about chess, I look it up and I can predict exactly how he will play the next time we meet.)

"You're right, so you go meet with them. Then before you are done, tell them you want to gather the house staff for a formal farewell before they leave for Altara. Tell them in the courtyard, mid-morning." he said.

"Where will you be?"

"I'll be watching over you," he said, cocking his head a little bit to indicate our previous spot overlooking the room.

I gave an unenthusiastic 'Okay' as I accepted my assignment to enter the lion's den as Anree.

"Mora, tell them I will be down in a few minutes," he said.

Looking from one of us to the other she said, "You know this is weird."

Together we said, "It sure is." Then we both cracked up.

After she left he gave me directions to the first floor entrance to the room. I guess I knew the way but I was so nervous I couldn't think straight. I tried to back out saying, "You go. I can't be you. What will I say?"

"Relax you are me. Remember two Taras, two Henrys. This is fun. The words will come to you. Their only power over you is the power you give them. One last thing my father always said, 'In unknown situations the less you say the more they will tell.' Make them fill the silence."

We left for our assignments, him to the safety of the overlook, I to the lion's den. As I went along the corridor I thought about how mature Anree seems. His confidence even in the face of challenging situations amazed me. I think he has such confidence because he really believes other people only have the power over you that you give them. Wow that's another rule. I will not give these people power over us.

I found the room. I started to knock, but I realized this was my house. I don't need permission to enter a room in my own house. (Except at home when my parent's bedroom door is shut, I knock. And Larry screams if I come into his room without permission, but too bad.)

I threw open the doors and walked up to the table. I immediately forgot the advice to keep my mouth shut and listen. I started talking, "Rosboes you gathered a good council here." I looked Rosboes straight in the eye as I spoke. Then I acknowledged each of the others by name, "Hara from Nork, Bar from Tran and Alrinar from Para."

93

Turning from Papo to Rosboes I continued, "Just the other day we were talking of you Papo, weren't we Rosboes. What was that about? (I paused just long enough, and then said.) Oh well, I don't recall."

Turning to Hara I said, "Hara, there are rumors in the house that you saw Candor in Nork while he was here with us. Surely it must have been a brother or cousin you saw." I shocked her by the direct challenge but I realized I might have said too much. Inside my head I shouted, 'shut up.' (Henry rule number 5, Note to self, Shut up.)

I needed to start them talking so I asked, "Can I do anything for you?"

I thought I heard Anree muffle a laugh upstairs, though none of them took their eyes off me, Rosboes spoke up, "Well we gathered to make sure everything goes well for the Gathering."

"And your plans are?" I asked.

They all waited for Rosboes to speak. "As always the first day will be the arrivals and the market, the second day we will honor the dead and raise the mound, the third day, the day of the Tara, and then the day of justice."

I nodded my head uncertain if this was the right order. I let there be silence. (I think I need to teach Fred about the silence.) I looked them each in the face and though my heart was pounding I remained calm and relaxed. "Are those your only plans?"

My question obviously struck at their conscience as they sat in silence looking anywhere but at me. Hara broke the silence, "We are wondering if you plan anything new when you become the Tara?"

I raised an eyebrow. I was growing comfortable with the silence.

Papo spoke next, "We are wondering if you want us to help you be the Tara?"

I raised my other eyebrow.

Bar spoke next, "Perhaps we could each help with justice in our own village. Perhaps we could be a council to you, you are so young."

I let there be silence. This silence stuff works. I could tell Bar regretted adding the 'so young' part. I broke my silence speaking softly, "I will give some thought to your ideas." I let there be a little more silence as though I was thinking about their ideas right then. I wanted to leave but I remembered what Anree wanted me to tell them. "I and the household staff would like to bid you a formal farewell tomorrow as you leave for Altara, about midmorning in the courtyard. I will travel on foot with the household the next day."

I stood up and turned to leave, but turning back I said, "I appreciate you taking the time to make all your plans for the Gathering and going early for preparations." They stared at me in silence. As I left I hoped Anree would stay to listen to their after talk.

Before I reached the door Rosboes called out, "Perhaps Candor would want to travel with us tomorrow and rejoin his brother and family at the Gathering." Rosboes said brother, with a tone indicating his doubts about the Candor story.

I turned back, "Oh thanks, but he is staying and traveling with me. I expect he will be with me

95

to say goodbye to you in the morning." As I went out the door I couldn't believe I said Candor would be there tomorrow.

I wanted to run back to the safety of our rooms, but there were people in the halls. If they saw Anree running from his meeting with Rosboes they would lose all confidence in him. I got lost trying to find my way back. Every turn I took put me in another unfamiliar hallway. It reminded me of those dreams where I'm at school and cannot find my classroom. I miss those dreams, but this is the most exciting thing I've ever done. When I finally got to our rooms, I fell on the cushions, exhausted.

Anree got back to the rooms about ten minutes after me. He burst into the room laughing. He joined me on the cushions on the floor, but he was still pumped up, "You were great. Just great. Everything you said was great. You are great. You are the one."

I was both thrilled and scared to death by his approval. I think I must tell Fred and Jamal and maybe even Larry how great they are sometime. I also wondered what Anree meant by, 'You are the one.'

"After I left what did they say?" I was anxious to learn how they reacted to my performance.

"First I had to stop myself from running right after you. You were so great. You're a better me than I am."

"Get to it, what did they say?" I asked, getting impatient.

"Okay, okay. They are a bit confused. Papo and Hara both said the boy Papo had in Para looked like me, but Papo admitted today was the first time he had seen me in a couple of years. He isn't sure we are identical."

"But I'm the boy he saw in Para and saw today," I said.

"I know, isn't it great, and Hara is still certain she saw Candor in Nork, but she isn't certain whether or not he has a brother. So now they have convinced themselves the boy in my room is the boy Papo found at Lothar, but they aren't absolutely certain we look alike. So then they went back and forth about what happens to their plan if there aren't two Taras at the Gathering. Also your little poke about 'all their plans' made them wonder what you know. They aren't really bad. They want more power and they think wealth will give them power."

"If not wealth, what then?" I was thinking in my world, wealth clearly equals power.

"My Father said people give you power. Everything is about the people. The people give you power and watch how you use it. These guys want to take the power away from the people by confusing them, like we just did to them."

"Do you think we took away their power," I said hoping the game was over.

"We confused them enough to shake their confidence. So right now yes we weakened them a bit, but the game will be decided when we find out if two Taras are more Tara or less Tara."

"What about the unicorn horn and the key?" I reminded him.

"I don't know about the key, but I have an idea about where to look for the horn. We'll search for it tomorrow after Rosboes and his friends leave."

I didn't say anything, but I had an idea about the key. A memory had been surfacing for a while. It was mid-afternoon and I wanted to go fishing. Anree thought leaving the house was risky, so we stayed in our rooms playing chess (I've been teaching him.) and swapping stories.

Anree carried on about how lucky I am to have a family and especially a little brother. He thinks Larry is the best part of my life, and when I see Larry through his eyes, I think he might be right. On the other hand I envy his independence and responsibility.

Chapter 14 Sunday Afternoon
The Real Tara

I got home at noon from going to church with Fred, to find out we were going to my grandparents for the afternoon. This is usually one of my least favorite ways to spend my afternoon. (My apologies to Granddad and Grandy.) However today, this was exactly what I wanted to do. I had even suggested the idea to Dad while we washed the car yesterday.

Ever since the first time I heard the similarity between Anree and Henry, I had been wondering something. I told you I'm named after a great-grandfather Henry who was an orphan. According to my father that's the entirety of the story, but I can remember at least once my Granddad telling a longer version of the story. And Anree's description of the keyhole stirred up other memories. (I guess you can see where I am expecting this will go?)

On the way in the car, Larry started whining about wasting his afternoon going to see our grandparents. Suddenly Dad turned around and shouted, "Grow up Larry, you don't always get to do what you want to do in life, and what's more the stuff you don't want to do is almost always more important than the stuff you want to do." He sounded so harsh everyone was quiet until we got to Granddad's house. I wondered if Dad was talking to himself or to Larry. I don't know if this is a rule or not, but I think it's true. I don't want to climb the rope, but I am going to try. I didn't want to go back to Altara, but I found Anree and he needed me. Dad's right, the stuff you don't want to do is more important than the stuff you want to do. (I still hate the rope. I think Dad had a particularly bad week at work last week.)

We had fried chicken for lunch. My Grandy makes the best fried chicken. Larry and I helped clear the table and do the dishes. Larry actually helped. Granddad went into the living room, turned on the TV and picked up the newspaper. Dad followed but picked up Grandy's laptop to run some system checks for her. Mom and Grandy stayed in the kitchen talking and making an apple pie.

Larry wanted to go outside, but I convinced him to follow me into the living room. For some reason I thought his presence would help.

"Granddad, will you tell me the story of great granddad Henry, the orphan one," I asked.

Granddad put down his paper, "Now that is a good story…."

Dad cut him off, "Don't bother your grandfather, you two go outside and play."

Granddad ignored him, "You boys come back to my room and we'll let your Dad work on the laptop."

I love Granddad's room. One half is a study with walls full of books and the other half is a workshop, with a drawing table and a work bench. He always has lots of projects going on. He been working on wood carving at one work bench and the drawing table was covered with pictures of birds.

"Your poor Dad, if it's not on a computer screen, he can hardly take it in. He's always been a genius with the computer. We gave him his first computer, a Commodore 64, when he was your age. What a wonderful Christmas morning. His eyes lit up he was so excited and by that evening he had opened up the case to see what was inside. Me, I like things I can touch. Now where is that?" He talked as he searched through drawers and cabinets.

I knew this was his way and somehow, whatever he was looking for would be part of what he would tell us.

He went on, "I wonder if your Dad has a box, maybe his computer is his box. I think every boy should have a box, a place for stuff, the kind you can't keep in your head. When you become a man, you should keep your box."

I have a box in my dresser drawer, with a pocketknife, my first watch, it no longer works, some of those coins you make by flattening pennies and a ball bearing. Yes, I have a box. I wonder if Larry has a box and if Anree has a box.

"Well now, here's the box I'm after." He sat down in his chair with a wooden box about the size of a three-inch thick notebook.

"I'm not certain how many greats ago, but about a hundred years ago, one of our grandfathers worked in the customhouse down by the docks. I think they use it for a visitor's center now. I went down there a few years ago." He paused as though thinking about going down there now.

"He was the orphan?" I asked trying to get him back to the story.

"No, he wasn't the orphan. He was married, but had no children. Now the docks were a busy place back then, with people coming and going all the time. A lot of immigrants arrived from Europe during those years."

"Every day our grandfather went home for lunch. One time, when he was heading back to the office, he saw a boy standing in the middle of the street about to be run over by a delivery wagon. Grandfather grabbed him and pulled him to the side of the street."

Granddad noticed Larry fidgeting, so he opened the box and pulled out a pocket watch. "I doubt this works but you might want it," he said handing the watch to Larry. My eyes turned green with envy.

Larry, who is always so eloquent, said, "Wow."

Obviously Granddad meant to amuse Larry with the watch so he could continue the story. "Grandfather couldn't get the boy to speak so he decided the boy must be from an immigrant family and he had gotten separated from them after they got off their ship. This often happened and sooner or later someone would come looking for the boy."

"Grandfather left him sitting on the front steps of the customhouse. All afternoon he sent people to talk to the boy. They tried every language they could think of German, French, Prussian, Lithuanian, Greek... The list goes on and on. They named every ship that had been in port. The boy still had no response. The boy sat out on the steps until the close of business and no one came for him. So, Grandfather took him home."

Larry started fidgeting again so Granddad pulled a gold chain out of the box to go with the watch. I almost screamed. I always thought Granddad favored Larry.

"Well, the boy was probably around Henry's age, but they couldn't get him to say a word. He would hardly eat anything. He wouldn't take off his clothes, and even though they put him in a bed at night, in the morning they found him sleeping on the floor."

"For the rest of the week, grandfather took the boy to the customhouse and sat him on the front steps. No one came for him. No one reported a missing boy. By the end of the week, grandmother had had enough of this and, when grandfather brought the boy home for lunch on Saturday, because back then they worked on Saturdays, grandmother kept the boy. She put him in a tub on the back porch, stripped off his clothes, and scrubbed him head to toe."

"Naked on the back porch," Larry exclaimed in amazement.

"Naked on the back porch," repeated Granddad, laughing at Larry's modesty. "When she finished, she burnt his clothes. She dressed him in clothes she bought that morning. Then she looked him straight in the face and said, 'Boy, tell me your name.' and the boy said 'Henry.' And so that's the story of your orphan grandfather Henry."

I let the silence hang for a few minutes, "When he was older did he ever talk about his former life. I mean if he was my age he would have remembered something."

"You know I've often thought that too, but if he did, nobody passed on that part of the story," Granddad said.

"People always leave out the good parts," Larry said.

I let it be silent again. Granddad opened the box, "There is one more little thing. Under his clothes Henry wore this key on this leather string. I showed it to a locksmith once. He said he had never seen a key like it. He offered me ten dollars for it. In fact you were with me Henry. You were four or five. We went to one of those Antique Treasure Searches at the museum. The guy in front of us had an antique padlock worth $500. Anyway I don't know what it opens but you can have it."

I knew immediately what it opened. I used all my self-control to stay in my chair, to not shout out "the Gates of Altara," to not grab the key but to wait until he handed it to me.

As I took the key, I realized I am descended from the missing Tara. All we needed now was the unicorn horn and Anree would be the full Tara. The night of the storm at Lothar, the hornless unicorn took Anree from Lothar to the street in front of the customhouse. When the boy finally said his name, 'Anree,' the grandmother heard Henry, and for some reason a hundred years later, the hornless unicorn came for me and carried me from my front yard back to Lothar.

"I can keep the key?" I asked barely able to contain my excitement.

"Yes, Larry can keep the watch and chain. You can keep the key," he said.

I kept turning it over in my hand. Finally I put the strap over my neck and slipped the key inside my shirt. When we left, I hugged Granddad and whispered 'Thanks' in his ear. I don't remember when I last hugged my Granddad.

As we drove home my internal celebration realized there was one big problem. I didn't know how to get the key to Altara.

Chapter 15 You are the Tara

I went to sleep with the key on the leather strap around my neck, but I woke in Altara without it. As I thought, getting the key to Altara would be a problem.

As soon as Anree woke I told him everything Granddad said.

He jumped to his feet shouting, "You are the Tara. You are the true Tara. The unicorn returned to the land and brought you. I want to shout it out the window."

I spent ten minutes settling him down. I used my words and as forcefully and as seriously as I could I said, "NO, NO, I'm Henry, I'm not the Tara. You are the Tara. You trained for the work and you are the Tara. Now we have almost everything we need to guarantee you are the true Tara."

"Well really we don't have anything we need or should I say you don't have anything you need to be the Tara." I stared at him, making it clear he wasn't funny, at all. He went on laughing and said. "Okay, we don't have the key and we don't have the horn. And how can the horse that brought you here be the hornless unicorn? How can the hornless unicorn still be alive a hundred years later? That really doesn't make sense."

"If the only part of this story that is hard to swallow is a hundred year old hornless unicorn, I think we will be doing fine," I said.

He laughed saying, "Hard to swallow, hard to swallow," over and over again and acting as if he was trying to choke down something. He knew how close I came to losing my temper and he wanted to get me in a better mood. But in truth I have grown up a lot since the day I jumped him as we returned from fishing.

When Mora brought our breakfast, Anree gave her instructions about gathering the household for a formal goodbye to Rosboes and his friends. She kept saying yes everything is ready as though they had already been over this several times.

We watched from our windows as everyone gathered in the courtyard. There were thirty people of the household and then Rosboes and friends. We put on matching hooded jackets like the one I wore as Candor.

"So what's the plan," I asked.

"We are going to go say goodbye," he said flipping up his hood and heading out the door.

I laughed a laugh of resignation knowing he had a plan. I would never let Fred or Jamal get away with acting this way.

When we got to the final hallway before stepping out of the building Anree told me to step out first and he would follow as Candor and depending on how things went we would reveal the two Taras.

I lead the way out the doors but Anree didn't follow. I found myself alone at the top of a set of stairs. The people of the household stood in front of me on the right and Rosboes' group sat on their horses to my left. Anree with his hood up finally came out the door to join me.

Rosboes called out, "Why does your friend Candor hide his face."

I started to make some excuse, but before I spoke he stepped past me and flipped back his hood and defiantly said, "I am not afraid to show my face. I do not hide."

This was not Anree. This must be the real Candor. He smiled at everyone and stepped back beside me. I think he was embarrassed to have spoken out so boldly to this group of adults. Anree was in the building behind us having the time of his life.

Mora was standing fairly near me, and since she didn't look weirded out, I was certain she assisted Anree with his surprise. She cleared her throat, which I took to mean, 'get it together and start talking.'

"I want to thank Alrinar of Para, Hara of Nork, Bar of Tran and of course our own Rosboes. They have worked hard on their plans for the Gathering." Turning to the household I said, "They leave us now to go start the Gathering at Altara and we are thankful."

Everyone stomped their feet in a sign of approval or agreement. If Mora's reports were true they were mostly celebrating the leaving part. When the stomping died down I continued, "Tomorrow I and my friend will join the household and their families in walking to Altara. Now before you go my dear Rosboes do you or your friends have anything you would like to say?"

Papo spoke up, "I want to thank you for the generosity of your house. And I want to say you have become a remarkable young ...," he paused for a moment then resumed, "you have become a remarkable man." The household went mad

108

stomping their feet. I think Papo was acknowledging we had won a victory or that we were a more formidable foe than they had realized.

When the noise died down I bid them farewell. "May the wind be with you in this and all your journeys."

The household started to disperse as the four conspirators rode out of the courtyard. I raised a hand asking them to wait. I was certain the show wasn't over but I wanted to make sure Rosboes' people were really gone.

I called out, "Would someone watch at the gates to make sure they don't turn back." I turned to the real Candor standing next to me, "Candor of Nork I assume?"

"You know I'm Candor. If you didn't know I was Candor why did you send for me in the middle of the night," he said sounding indignant, confused and tired. I hugged him. He pushed me away.

With perfect timing Anree came out the doors with his hood up. When everyone could see him, he flipped it back. Candor almost fell over in shock.

Mora must have warned the members of the household. They stomped their feet, in salute and joy.

When they settled down I took the lead speaking, "There are two Taras, before the week is done, we will restore the fullness of the Tara, the fullness of Altara."

Anree completed my thought saying, "Tell people, the Tara is twice the person they think he is."

"We leave for Altara at dawn tomorrow," I added.

Everyone stomped their feet and cheered.

Candor followed us back up to our rooms. Anree alternated between Candor and me saying, "You should have seen your face."

Candor kept saying, "I don't understand."

Anree's joking made me feel bonded with Candor, when we got to our rooms I said to Candor, "It's like this, there was a boy named Henry and a boy named Anree and they met, and they were identical. They talked and talked and soon there were two Anrees and two Henrys, but still only two boys." As I said this I realized, only a couple of days before, I had gotten mad at Anree over this idea.

"But who is who?" Candor asked, looking from one of us to the other.

"That's the point, there is no difference," Anree said.

I thought to myself there is no difference except before this is done I'll see you raised up as the Tara and I will be Henry on Fire in Suborediom with my family. Then I wondered if Anree had his own plan for how the week would end. We share memories, but we don't seem to share all thoughts and particularly not future plans. I wish a one hundred year old hornless unicorn was the only difficult thing to explain.

Anree took a small wooden chest from a cabinet in one of the other rooms. He said, "This box belonged to the Tara. I thought about it when Henry talked about his Granddad's box." He pulled out a set of keys. "I bet one of these is the key to Rosboes' rooms."

Grabbing the keys and heading for the door I said, "The search is on."

Anree tells Candor, "We are looking for a unicorn horn."

"You're looking for what?" Candor was behind me as we ran through the halls, so I couldn't see his face, but he must have thought we were crazy.

As we arrived at the door to Rosboes room I told Candor, "The night the child went missing the hunters cut the horn from the unicorn. That's why the unicorn left Altara."

One of the keys got us in the door. There were two rooms. As you would expect the front room had a seating area, a fireplace and a table with two chairs. The back room was a bedroom. We searched both rooms. After two hours we had looked through everything twice. We plopped down on the sofa and chairs in the seating area.

"We need to think this through," I said.

Candor was laid back on the sofa and without even opening his eyes said, "It's about time someone did some thinking."

"Do you remember the other day Rosboes said something about the unicorn," Anree started.

"He said it was a myth, or a story." I finished. "He didn't say they are gone or they aren't here anymore, he said they were never here."

"So if he has the horn he doesn't know it," Anree said.

Candor reconnected, "How long has Rosboes had these rooms?"

"He and his father before him have lived here since this part of the house was built," Anree answered.

Candor got up to look at two unicorns carved into the stone fireplace mantle. They faced each other. The unicorn was used as a decoration throughout the house. Candor focused on tracking where the horns pointed. We followed the line from each horn to a point on the opposite wall near the ceiling. We got the chairs from the table to get a closer look. We found nothing. We checked the place on the wall where the two lines crossed and again nothing. We fell back on the furniture.

After about ten minutes Candor spoke. Still focusing on the unicorns on the mantle he said. "The horns on these unicorns are a bit big for the size of their bodies."

"So," one of us said.

"Well also everything about the two animals is the same, except the horn on the right is slightly larger than the horn on the left," he said.

At this we all three stood up to look more closely at the horn on the right. A knife, almost a small sword, leaned against the mantel. About an inch was broken off the tip but it still worked to chisel around the horn. The material around the horn wasn't stone, it was plaster. In less than fifteen minutes we held an eighteen-inch unicorn horn in our hands passing it from one to another.

When I held the horn, the Fire in me burned as hot as a bed of coals. I filled with sorrow from the horrible act committed against this animal a hundred years ago. And suddenly I filled with memories of all the times I have been a jerk for no reason. I passed the horn on to Candor. I wondered if the horn had the same effect on Anree and Candor. This was the real Taking. The people took something they had absolutely no right to take. This truly needed to be undone. And yet we could not put the horn back. How could we undo this?

We headed back to our rooms with our new found treasure. We ran into Mora on the way. Anree hid the horn.

"I've been looking all over the house for you. Candor's parents expect him to be at the camp outside Altara tonight and there is a group leaving now he can travel with."

We all hugged. (I would never hug Fred or Jamal.) We thanked Candor for his help and asked him not to tell too much to anyone. He said nobody would believe half of what he had seen and done here.

Back in our rooms we laid on the cushions passing the horn back and forth. "Now, the problem is how we get the key here."

Anree passed me the horn. "Maybe the unicorn could go for it."

"Well that is what has to happen but how do we do that?"

"The other thing I'm thinking is we might not have found the horn without Candor. Maybe we need another person to bring us the key," Anree said.

"Maybe one of the guides could go for it if we had the unicorn."

Anree says, "I could go for it if we had the unicorn."

"Maybe I can try again to bring it." (The idea of Anree going to my world gives me the shivers. That doesn't seem very fair does it? I'm reading Treasure Island for a book report. I like it because it's written in first person like a journal. Anyway the boy, Jim Hawkins, stops by his mother's inn on the way to go to sea and meets the boy she hired to do his job at the inn while he is gone. He immediately dislikes the boy and gives him all kinds of things to do and tells him he does everything wrong. Anree has no trouble sharing his life with me, but the smallest thought of him in my world makes me feel like Jim Hawkins seeing the other boy do his job.)

Before we went to sleep we packed shoulder bags with clothes and sleeping rolls for our journey to the Gathering.

Chapter 16 Monday Morning
The End is in Sight

While on the bus to school, I figured out everything will be over on Thursday. I guess really Thursday night when I'm in Altara. That's when Anree will become the Tara or he won't. I'm not physically tired, but somewhere deep inside, I'm exhausted and yet I am feeling alive in a new way. Both these lives are real. I am certain I live here and dream of my life in Altara, but I am also certain I live in Altara with Anree and dream of my life with Mom and Dad and Larry. In neither life do I ever really sleep.

This week I have the Treasure Island book report due on Wednesday and a quiz using the volume formulas in geometry. Oh yes, and Friday the rope. I guess it all wraps up in Altara Thursday night and in gym class Friday with the rope.

Jamal posted on Facebook last night saying he and Angela would be 'dining together' at lunch and Fred posted that he was playing Tervel in chess. I spent lunch reading Treasure Island. I wrote Tanya and asked if she would have lunch with me on Wednesday.

After writing all through lunch, I stopped by the table where Fred and Tervel were playing chess. Tervel is a natural. He definitely had the upper hand in their game. I asked them to watch my books while I went to the restroom. I just left my books on the table. I must have done this a hundred times before and never thought a thing about it. Anyway I came out of the restroom and suddenly thought, 'My journal is on top of all my other books, but Fred wouldn't open my books. Fred would respect my privacy.' As soon as I thought that, I started running back to the table to find Fred reading the pages I had just finished writing.

Inside my head I was saying, 'Now Henry, be calm. Let's not get another detention.' I was calm, very calm.

Fred committed the crime of the century, but he innocently said, "Wow this is great! You're writing fantasy fiction. What kind of place is Altara?"

All I could think was 'the calmer I am the less interested he will be.' But really all I did was tell the truth, "Really it's a lot like here."

"Why? If I was going to make up a fantasy world I would have a big sword and there would be dragons and maybe some talking animals and definitely some type of flying horses to ride when I fought the dragons and maybe a crossbow would be better than a sword, maybe I would ride the dragons and fight the people who rode the flying horses." he said and closed my journal. He headed off to class acting as if he was part of an invisible sword fight.

Fred was right, if I was making up a fantasy world, I would have included some of those things he talked about, but the most unusual part of my story is a one hundred year old hornless unicorn. Oh and my identical other with whom I share memories. (Did I use whom right? As I keep saying, I can only tell you what happens. I could never make this stuff up. I'm glad you are still reading.)

Tanya was waiting for me at my bus after school. Silly me, I smiled when I saw her. She stuck a note in my hand and walked away dramatically, something between striding and stomping. Notes are just a primitive form of text messaging, but I am about as far away from having a cell phone as I am from driving.

I sat down on the bus and began to unfold the note. Girls always find the most complicated way to fold notes. The entire message said, "You are obviously too busy for a social life. Good bye." She didn't even sign it.

She sucked the Fire out of me. This relationship stuff is a lot of trouble. So maybe she didn't see the email I sent last night, the one about lunch on Wednesday or maybe she saw it and thought we should have lunch on Monday. As soon as I got home I ran to check my email, but Mom caught me and I had to do chores. Monday is dusting and then she made sure I did homework. When I finally got to the computer there was an email from Tanya.

Dear H

> I didn't see your email until I got home today. You need to decide if you really have time for a relationship. If you had a cell phone this would be so much easier. Fred and Jamal say you are obsessed with writing. And Fred said you practically had a meltdown when you found him reading your stuff. What are you writing? I tried keeping a diary but every day I wrote the

same thing. But I guess now that we are dating I might have more to tell my diary. I could tell it about you. I wouldn't let you read it though. Today I would write, 'Henry needs to decide if he really cares about me." T

I took a breath. I was mad, but I was not sure whether I was mad at her or myself or Fred. I could see she was online, which meant she could see I was online, so she had to be wondering why I was not writing back. I decided to ignore all her questions.

Hi T

I am sorry I've been distracted. So how about lunch on Wednesday? H

Hi H

So I guess you're not going to tell me what you are writing, which is fine. We've only been out twice, so it's not as if you owe me an explanation of anything. I was talking to Angela after fifth period and she says I am getting too carried away with all this any way. And that a lot of it is just that middle school boys aren't very mature, but I said you were serious and mature. I hope you are because I am not going to invest in a relationship if you're not. I don't see why we can't do lunch Tuesday? T

I started thinking about the phrase, 'invest in a relationship'. We are in middle school, what does invest in a relationship mean? I wrote back,

Hi T

Tuesday it is. H

118

Hi H

Well that will work great. So lunch Tuesday and Wednesday it is. Come by my locker on the way to lunch. You know if I had your combination I could leave my math book in your locker and pick it up later in the afternoon. Any way we can talk about all this tomorrow. Angela and I are going to the mall later and buy some nail polish. I'm thinking of getting a deep magenta. Every time I paint my toe nails I do a different color. Maybe I just haven't found my signature color yet. Maybe today I will.   T

I wrote back a simple, 'see you at lunch.' But in my head I was screaming, 'What is going on.' I have so much to learn about girls. I am certain I have the most boring life in all Suborediom and now Tanya and also Anree are both trying to move in with me.

The rest of the evening was uneventful. I went to bed with the key tied around my wrist.

Chapter 17 No Key for Altara

Dawn was breaking out our east windows when I woke up and I could hear people in the courtyard below.

We washed, grabbed our bags and headed downstairs. Over a hundred people were already gathered in the courtyard. Thirty people work in the house. Some live in the house, some live nearby. Their families and other people from Roan made up the rest of the group.

As we came out of the house, the crowd grew silent and then, as if by a signal, they all began to stomp and cheer. Mora ran up to us, "Everyone is going to the Gathering. People are saying a new age has come to Altara. People are excited, but me, I'm frightened. I'm very frightened."

"I know Mora, I'm a little frightened too. A lot is going on, maybe more than we know." Anree said.

Out of a reflex I looked at my wrist as though checking a watch. I realized I was checking for the key. We have only two or three days before we have to have the key, and as of now we have no idea of how to get it.

Anree and I began to move through the crowd together. People touched us and blessed us. Memere kissed each of us and clasped her hands to her chest.

Memere and other older people rode on a wagon. The rest of us set off walking. Anree had gotten walking sticks for us and we wore shirts without hoods. We had agreed we would no longer hide. The Taras would walk together in the open. A spirit of hope and optimism filled the people as we began our journey. Our numbers grew to more than two hundred as we left town.

Throughout the morning as we walked along, people came up to us to plead their case. Bartese and his wife Tessa approached us saying, "We are so blessed to have two Taras."

"Yes, twice blessed," echoed Tessa.

"I am still the son of a Tara for a few more days," I said.

"Yes, yes, but we are so blessed. I am so blessed, but I have one little problem I want to tell to the Tara," Bartese went on.

"Now my good Bartese, after the ceremony we will sit and hear cases," Anree said.

"Yes, yes, but this is so small I do not need a full judgment. I do not need all the ceremony. My problem is so small. I would not even bother you if I could solve my problem some other way."

"Okay Bartese, tell us about this little problem weighing so heavily on you." I said.

"Yes, Yes, I will tell you. My neighbor is stealing our chickens and I need you to tell him to pay us for them," Bartese pled. His wife next to him nodded vigorously.

"Now how can I know what is right if I do not also hear from your neighbor." Obviously Bartese had hoped to declare this a small problem and somehow get a judgment from the Tara without his neighbor's side being heard.

"Our neighbor is a liar and a thief," Tessa said adamantly.

"Tarkan, is your neighbor right?" Anree said.

"Yes, yes, he's my neighbor," Bartese said.

"And he has been your neighbor since before we were born," I said.

"Yes, at least twice that time," Tessa said.

"Has he always been a liar and a thief?" Anree asked.

"No, not always," Tessa admitted reluctantly.

"So really he is your friend," Anree said.

"Yes, a friend who is a liar and a thief." He was softening a little bit.

"After the ceremony, I will sit down with you and your friend and we will find out about those chickens," I said.

Bartese and Tessa went away satisfied.

Not twenty minutes later, Sartan came along side us. He did not even pause to say hello, before he started pleading his case. "The corner spot in the market has always been my spot."

"Always?" I asked.

"For a long time. Now Dirk gets there very early and takes my spot. No one even wants his baskets, but all day he is in my spot."

"You could go earlier to the market," Anree said.

"I would have to sleep in the market to be earlier than him," Sartan complained.

"After the ceremony, I will sit with you and Dirk, and you will talk and he will talk and we will talk," I said.

So it went all morning. The wonderful thing was everyone loved Anree. No, to be honest, they loved us. No one tried to figure out who was the new Anree or the real Anree. Just as Anree had said, there were two Anrees and two Taras. Together we were stronger than anyone expected.

Together we were the Fire of Altara. I just wasn't sure how much Henry was here.

At noon we stopped for lunch. Everyone offered us some of their food, but we ate with Memere. After lunch most people rested, but Anree and I played a ball game with some younger kids. We used a cork ball to play a game like soccer. The ball went off the field into a group of adults. One of the kids chased after it, but before he reached it someone kicked it across the field and into some trees. This time I went after it.

I was twenty feet into the woods when a guy wearing a mask stepped out from behind a tree. Nothing about him looked familiar. He held up a large knife. In a disguised voice he said, "Some of us think two Taras are two to many and they sent me to start whittling down the number."

I turned and ran, running into Anree before I made it out of the woods.

He said, "I sensed something was wrong."

"I'd say so. A guy with a knife said he was sent to reduce the number of Taras starting with me."

Anree didn't even hesitate, "Come on," and we headed back into the woods. There was no sign of the guy. We found the kids ball and took it back to them. We then started walking through the camp to see if we could spot the guy, but we now numbered around five hundred and we couldn't find him. We chose not to tell anyone.

During the afternoon we walked beside the wagon with the older people. The kids we played ball with tagged along beside us so we asked the people on the wagon to tell the stories of Altara. Each story took a long time because, they argued among themselves about the details of the stories, but here are final versions of two of the stories.

The River Al

Many years ago the sea was very far away and the land was very dry. The land begged the sea to come closer and water the land, but the seawater was very salty and only made the land thirstier. So the land begged the sky to send water and quench the thirst of the land, but the sky had no water to spare. So the land begged the mountain to send water to quench its thirst. For twelve days the land pleaded for water and for twelve days the mountain said no. Then on the twelfth day the sorrow of the land was so great it broke the heart of the mountain to say no. When the heart of the mountain broke, the side of the mountain shook and rumbled and opened. The river Al poured forth out of that opening, out of the very heart of the mountain. The river flowed through the land quenching its thirst and filling the sea and giving water to the sky for rain. The place where the heart of the mountain broke is Lothar.

The woman speaking covered her mouth when she said Lothar, as though the word would hurt us and remind us there is no real Tara.

I reached over and took her hand. "Everything will be okay. The broken heart will be healed. We will heal the broken heart of the land." Anree and I both knew this was a big promise. Her eyes welled up with tears and so did ours.

Anree put everybody back in a good mood by calling out, "Another story. Tell the story of the first Tara."

The First Tara

The Tara was born when the land was born. When the River Al came down from the mountain, the Tara took a stick and drew the path for the river to follow from the mountain to the sea. The Tara found himself on one side of the River and unable to get to the other side because the River was so deep and so wide. He did not yet know how to swim. He was happy though and saw no need to cross the river until one day a woman appeared on the other side of the river. He had never seen a woman before and he thought she was beautiful. He wanted to talk to her. If he walked up the river toward the mountain, she walked up her side of the river toward the mountain. And if he walked toward the sea she walked toward the sea, but he could find no way to cross the river. Finally he decided to build a boat. It took him twelve days to cut down trees and build a boat. And in the boat he crossed the river to meet the woman. They made their home in Altara the place of the Gathering. Her name was Talara.

So we passed the afternoon walking and listening to stories. When the day grew dark, we camped under the stars. Many people brought us food insisting theirs was the best. Finally we were so full, we hid so people would quit feeding us.

Our plan for the evening was to sleep in a tree. We set up a tent with our sleeping mats and stuff

125

to look like we were under the blankets. We quietly slipped away to the edge of the camp. We had borrowed two coils of rope. Up in the tree Anree quickly made each of us a rope basket like I had napped in at the Well of the Wind. Hopefully we had done all this unnoticed and could sleep in safety. Tonight I fell asleep with images of the man with the knife.

Chapter 18 Tuesday Morning
No Time for Henry

Everything piled up on me today. Instead of a journal I need a calendar. I was so obsessed over things going on in Altara I lost track of what was happening here.

I'm sure you remember that last night, I made a lunch date with Tanya for today and for tomorrow. Well I forgot I also had the chess game with Coach today. At least I forgot until Fred reminded me at the bus stop. I barely walked up before he started.

"So did you sleep well?" He asked.

"I slept about as well as usual." I said, trying to figure out why he asked and wondering if this had anything to do with Altara.

"So you're ready?" he said.

I got aggravated and sharply asked, "Ready for what?"

"For the rematch, don't tell me you forgot? Have you even thought about a first move? Do you have a strategy? You had a weak opening in the last game and I hoped you would think through your mistakes. Henry, you have been somewhere else for the past week. What is wrong with you?" I wanted to be mad at Fred, but I was really mad at myself. I am the one who messed up. Fred is worried about climbing the rope. He is more worried than I am. I continue to increase my number of chin-ups. As soon as I sat down on the bus I also remembered my lunch date.

After morning classes I had a few minutes to find Tanya, beg off lunch and go meet Coach for our chess game. I found her at her locker and we walked toward the cafeteria together.

"I'm sorry about not seeing your email and giving you that nasty note," she said.

"The note wasn't so nasty."

"I meant it to be," she said laughing.

"Maybe I'm thick skinned."

"Or thick headed. So what are you writing? When can I read it?"

She is so ready to walk right into my life. "I'm not sure about letting anyone read it. I'll be done in a few days."

"So you'll be done tomorrow?" She persisted.

I think her understanding of 'a few' is interesting. 'A few' is definitely more than one, if I meant one, I would say tomorrow. Saying 'a few' is about leaving open wiggle room. I decided not to point this out to her.

"Probably not tomorrow, possibly on Friday," I'm trying to be vague.

"Is it an extra credit report? I know Angela and Jamal go in for all that stuff. I do in social studies, but that's it. If it's social studies, I could help."

Her offer of help felt genuine and I wanted help. At least at some level, I wanted someone's help, but I told her no. Deep down I'm scared. I'm scared Anree and Altara will go away.

"It's not even a school thing. I'm doing it for me." I was hoping she would let it go.

"If that's how it is, then that's how it is. Anyway I forgot I promised to have lunch with Angela so maybe I will see you later," and she left.

I was stunned and trying to figure out what happened. Instead of me standing her up for lunch, she stood me up, and instead of her being mad at me for forgetting our lunch date she was mad at me because I won't share what I am writing. Now I'm hurt at being dumped on a lunch date I couldn't keep.

My first serious boy-girl relationship hit a rough spot today. Anyway at least I was free for the chess game.

A small crowd was already around our table when I got to the cafeteria. A couple of the football players, Randy and Kenny, sat on either side of Coach. He had been explaining to them how chess taught him to think ahead and to think strategically. Middle school football players are the guys who have started to grow and who are less clumsy than the rest of us. Kenny is okay and sharp in math. Randy can, at times, be a bully and I avoid him.

Fred was right in the last game I had a weak opening and I underestimated my opponent. Today I had a clear plan to establish and maintain control of the center of the board. I won't bore you with all the moves. I think Jamal memorized them so if you want to know a blow-by-blow account you can ask him, but I will give you a few highlights.

My strategy developed well until I left one of my pawns unprotected. Coach took it with his queen's bishop and then retreated. My control was weakened. I took a pawn and a knight from him, but he took my king's bishop. Things progressed and I thought we were heading for another draw but he slipped and left his queen open. I took her and in four moves had checkmate.

The game was challenging until I took his queen. On one hand he may have made a mistake yet, on the other, I wondered if he gave it to me. Jamal watches football on TV. Sometimes, he complains that his team had a bad win. I always think, 'Why aren't you glad they won?' He always explains they won not because they played well, but because the other team messed up. Well this was a weak win. Fred could not contain himself. He kept hollering, "No Rope! No Rope!" Noticing my more subdued response, Coach leaned over and said, "And no rope for you, too. Aren't you happy?"

"I guess I'm learning that just because something is hard, and I might fail at it, is not a reason not to try."

"Henry Miller you seem to be growing up fast. Is everything okay?"

"Yeah it's okay," and shook his hand.

Between Tanya and writing, I am way behind on reading Treasure Island. I am only three fourths of the way through the book. The report has to be three pages and is due tomorrow. As I read, I identify more and more with Jim Hawkins and his adventure. Like I said the day piled up on me and it was my fault.

Chapter 19
The Key is Trapped in Suborediom

I woke up stiff from sleeping in the tree, but alive. (Always a good way to start the day.) I announced to Anree, "Again no key."

"We are going to need help I tell you," he said.

"Calling all unicorns, calling all unicorns," I said laughing.

"Maybe," he said not laughing.

Our tent had been ransacked and slashed during the night so obviously someone came looking for us. We still told no one, though some people saw the tent. More people joined the encampment during the night and wanted to greet the two Taras. We walked through the areas where they camped. They clasped our hands. Some stared in amazement. We kept our eyes open for the man with the knife.

On the road several groups on horseback passed us during the morning. Merchants with carts and horses piled with goods now traveled with us.

About midmorning one of these peddler couples came alongside us. They seemed to be positioning themselves to plead their case. The other travelers naturally fell away to give these people some privacy. Their animal, though tall at the shoulder, walked as though carrying a great burden. The poor horse held his head bent to the ground and was covered with blankets. The merchants, a man and woman, were similarly down trodden.

When we had sufficient distance from the other travelers Anree spoke to them. He assumed them to be older and addressed them saying, "Now Mother and Father, surely the burden on your heart is no greater than the burden you have put on the back of this poor animal."

Without raising her head the woman spoke saying, "We bear not a burden, but a gift for the Taras."

"Thanks for your generosity, but now is not the time for gifts." As I spoke I knew pushing away their gift was wrong. If they wanted to give us a gift we should accept it, but they seemed so poor I could not imagine accepting anything from them.

"We bring you a treasure. A treasure I believe you seek," the man said.

We walked in silence for a while. I tried to imagine what treasure they brought. Anree had the unicorn horn in his bag. The key was at home in my room. Finally I asked, "You bring us a treasure?"

"You look upon us, but do not see," the woman said.

Anree grew hotly impatient with this exchange. Maybe while I had become more 'Anree' he had become more 'Henry.' Very strongly he said, "So what do you hide?"

"We hide many things," the man said. Then the two peddlers raised their heads and stood up straight. As they straighten up it was as if a veil had lifted. They were the guides Kur and Lara. They slouched back into their previous appearance and were once again the old man and the old woman. I was so thankful to count them among the good guys, but I stayed calm in order to not draw attention to us. "There are many reasons to hide one's face," Lara said smiling at us.

Anree also immediately recognized them. "Yes, many reasons."

"We no longer hide, we walk in the open." I said.

"Oh, that is known the full length of the Al, from Lothar to Rahtol," Kur said.

"And you, why do you now hide?" Anree asked.

"We hide, in order to bring you what you seek," Kur said. He reached over and turned back part of the blanket covering the horse's forehead, revealing the scar. Their horse was the hornless unicorn.

I reached out and touched the scar, the place where the horn had been cut from his forehead. I filled with all the pain and sorrow of this creature, but the pain was also the pain of this land, these people. Opening the gates would be a symbolic act, but if we could heal this wrong, we would change the story of the people of Altara. Anree lifted my hand off the scar and covered it back up and we stood in silence. We felt the pain differently. Anree lived with this sorrow throughout his life, even if he did not know it. However, to me the pain was new and powerful. The pain throbbed within me. Anree hugged the unicorn's neck and whispered something in his ear. Then we walked away.

"What did you whisper in his ear?" I asked.

"You didn't realize I spoke unicorn did you."

"You don't speak unicorn. If you did who would you talk to?"

Anree tilted his head towards where Kur and Lara and the unicorn walked with the other travelers.

"If you spoke unicorn, I would speak unicorn." He remained silent with a smug look on his face. "You're not going to tell me are you?"

"Nope," he said laughing.

"You are not as funny as you think you are," I said.

"No, but we sure have fun together don't we," he said.

"I guess we do."

We arrived at Altara at midday. When I actually saw Altara, the Gathering place, I finally understood that when all the people gathered here this was the land.

Altara is an enormous parkland that for this week, became a tremendous city. The road had slowly been climbing up from the river and now we were on a plain that on one side dropped a hundred feet back down to the river. We enter on a narrow roadway passing between two large ponds. Fish jumped and turned along the surface of the water. The roadway led up to and around the locked gates of Altara.

Two dozen earthen mounds had been raised above the plain. Flat on top, some were a few feet high and some as tall as a three or four story building. The top of one was as large as a football field. Some had buildings and tents on top of them.

Thousands of people filled the area. Past the gates an enormous market was spread out. The people, who had been walking near us on the road, all knew where to go as they arrived. As we passed through the crowd making our way toward our mound, people made way for us, but they also reached out to touch us.

Our mound towered over the other mounds, at least twenty feet taller than the nearest competitor. Logs set into the side created a stairway. We would live in the small house on top for the next few days. We could view the whole gathering from the top of our mound. I wish I could describe everything. There were encampments where people lived, a large cooking area, games or contests of various types happening on different mounds, corrals for the horses. I had never seen anything like the mounds or all the people, or the whole Gathering.

We spent a half hour taking in the sights. Anree pointed to other mounds and told me stories of each one. As he talked I remembered more and more. Rosboes, Hara, Bar and Papo showed up interrupting our time and our mood.

Rosboes shouted, "May we come up."

"Certainly," I called back. The six of us sat in a circle on the ground.

After a few pleasantries about our journey and the size of the Gathering, Rosboes got down to business. "So which of you is Candor?"

He spoke to us as though we were children he caught misbehaving. Neither Anree nor I were shaken by his tone.

"Obviously neither of us is Candor. You met Candor in Roan just a day ago. He looks nothing like us," Anree said.

Trying a different tone and a different question, Papo asked, "Which of you did the unicorn bring to Lothar?"

"Unicorn? I thought unicorns only appeared in stories told to children." I said looking at Rosboes as I echoed his words.

"The word throughout the Gathering is that by a long and torturous journey the hornless unicorn of ancient story brought the second Tara from beyond the sea," Papo said.

"That is quite a story," was all I managed to say. I imagined Candor had supplied the part about the hornless unicorn, but I could not imagine where the rest of the story came from. They carefully examined us, trying to find anything to separate us, one from the other. As I have said before we are identical, and of course Anree jumped in to explain.

"We are not one and then another." I am beginning to enjoy the faces people make as Anree gives this explanation. "We are one who is two."

"Don't be silly boy," Rosboes said.

Rosboes dismissal served to empower us. The Fire grew strong in me and in Anree also. Anree said in a polite, but dismissing way, "Rosboes, you have served well these years as guardian, but the time has come to let go."

"Do you plan to be the Tara together?" asked Hara.

"I'm not sure how that will work out, but I'm willing to wait and see. Are you?" I asked.

Bar took a turn. "I hear that after we left Roan, you told people the true Tara would be restored."

"Yes, the Tara, will no longer be the descendent of the brother of the Tara. He will be the true Tara," I said.

"How can that be?" Bar asked.

"I don't know how, but it will be," I said.

"I value your council and the Tara wants your help in serving the people of Altara." Anree said.

"Will you pledge to serve the Tara and the people of Altara?" I asked.

"If the true Tara shows up we will pledge to him." Rosboes said and the others nodded. He emphasized the word 'true' to imply we were not.

"Then this will be a great Gathering," Anree said.

With a tone of warning Rosboes says, "You need more than clever words and confusing ideas to become the true Tara."

"Yes, we will need much more," I said.

The council of four left. We sat in silence for a while, resting from the exchange. Anree spoke, "Do you think they will try anything?"

"I don't think they are done trying, and there is still the guy with the knife. I do think we have won the love of the people. We carry no weapons or wealth, no insignia of office. We are not the oldest or the wisest or the strongest. We have none of the things I would call the trappings of power and yet I feel as though we are riding the crest of a great wave of power." I said.

137

"Did I forget to mention how my father said, 'The river flows always to the sea, but not so the wind or the affections of the people,'" Anree said.

"Yeah you forgot to mention that one."

Trying to recapture a lighter mood Anree said, "Any chance we are the best looking."

"Afraid not," I said.

Anree and I spent the rest of the day touring the market. The food, the weave of the baskets, the cloth and leatherwork all excited and interested us. People loved explaining to us their secret techniques that made their goods the best. We asked questions, complimented people's work and tasted things more mysterious and definitely more wonderful than cafeteria food. The people were as interested in us as we were in the items and foods in the market. Rosboes, Hara, Bar and Papo also passed through the market talking to whoever would listen. They grew quiet whenever we came near. They wanted to recruit supporters. At one point they were talking to four men, anyone of which could have been the man with the knife. Anree thought they were Rosboes cousins from Rahtol.

After the market we went to an area on the edge of the mound city where people filled baskets with dirt. We pitched in to help. I don't mean to be slow, but at first I thought we were digging a new fishpond, but I realized more importantly we were gathering dirt to build or raise a mound higher. I don't know how many basket and bags Anree and I filled, but I worked hard and sweated hard.

Chapter 20 Wednesday Morning
A Final Relationship Report

First thing this morning Larry knocked on my door. My door was open and I couldn't for the life of me figure out why he would be knocking instead of barging in. Then I noticed he looked scared.

"Can I talk to you about something?" he asked hesitantly.

"Sure," I said continuing to get dressed.

"Last night," he said followed by a long pause.

"Yes, last night?" I was wondering how long he would drag this out.

"Last night I woke up in the middle of the night and there was a horse looking in my window," he said.

Now he had my attention. "Did he have a white spot on his forehead?"

"How did you know?"

"I just knew. Go on, what happened?"

"The horse didn't scare me," Larry said.

"What scared you?"

"I came to tell you and you weren't here. I searched the whole house, you weren't here," I started to panic. "Did you wake Mom and Dad?"

"No, and I'm not going to tell," he said.

"Good, what happened to the horse?"

"The horse was gone when I went back to bed. Where were you?" he asked.

"I can't tell you now. I'll tell you later. Now I have to run or I'll miss the bus. Don't tell anyone, anything and I will tell you more about the horse this afternoon." Then I grabbed my books and ran out the door without breakfast. I hadn't finished my book report and I planned to finish on the way to school.

On the bus Fred kept calling me a slacker, for finishing my book report on the bus. I told him I'm not a slacker I just have a very full life. He laughed.

In my book report I wrote about Jim Hawkins and his maturity. (Maturity is a current vocabulary word.) Jim, on his own, acted very resourceful and mature. However, when he was with the adults, whether it's Long John Silver and the pirates or with the good guys, he was a kid again. I feel much the same way. When in Altara I act grown up and mature, but at home or at school I'm goofy Henry. (Of course I didn't talk about Altara in my report.)

In the hallway on the way to first period, Tanya passed me a note. The note was rather longer than necessary, but it came down to finally say Gwen texted Tanya on the way to school telling her that Angela and Jamal had broken up, so she and Gwen are having lunch with Angela to help her through this tragic time. The note ended by saying, 'If you are lucky, I will see you for a few minutes at the end of lunch, look for me.' I was glad to have the time to myself.

I spent lunch alone and writing. I never even thought of looking up Jamal and asking if he was okay after his break up with Angela. Tanya found me at the end of lunch. As she came up to the table, I gave her an Anree smile, but it had no effect on her. When she reached my table she immediately announced, "All boys are pigs. Angela is done with Jamal. Gwen is done with Fred and I'm done with you," then she walked away. I had no idea what I did or did not do. On reflection I think my first boy-girl relationship went pretty well. It almost lasted a week.

First thing when Larry got home he headed to my room.

"So, what about the horse? Where were you?" He asked.

I had not figured out an answer or even decided what to tell him or how he could help. I wanted to talk to Anree about this. So I came up with this lame idea, "You know Larry, I think you dreamed the horse and me being gone."

"So why did you say you would tell me about it later? And why did you say not to tell anyone?"

"Okay you're right, you're right. I just can't have you telling Mom and Dad and I can't tell you what's up until maybe Friday. If I give you ten bucks, it's all I have, will you stay quiet?" I was pleading.

With a hurt look he said, "I'll stay quiet because you're my brother." I felt wounded. Anree was right about little brothers. I felt better when he added, "But I guess I would take five to remind me to be quiet."

I gave him the five and gave him a friendly shuffle with my knuckles on his head.

In the evening I worked on my geometry homework. I had been trying to figure how much dirt made up our mound at Altara. And then I wanted to figure how many baskets of dirt it took to build the mound. My textbook didn't have a formula for this so I went on line to find the formula for the volume of a trapezoid. I finally figured out the mound was a truncated square pyramid. (Okay, technically this was not working on my homework.) With that information I found a formula.

The formula was Volume=1/3(a squared + a times b + b squared) x h where a equal the length of the square on top and b equal the length of the square on bottom and h equal the height of the pyramid. So I estimated the mound Anree and I lived on as 50 ft. high (=H), 100 yards square at the base (=b) and 30 yards square at the top (=a). So that would be:

(8100 + 27,000 + 90,000)x50/3
(125,100)x50/3
6,255,000/3
= 2,085,000 cubic feet

When we filled baskets for the mound raising, I estimated each person could carry one and a half cubic feet of dirt. So our mound is made up of about 1,390,000 basket loads of dirt. Who said math wasn't useful? The raising of the mounds in Altara was an amazing task. Now I'm going to do my real homework and then go to sleep.

Chapter 21
Gathering the Dead in Altara

At mid-morning we all gathered around a large low mound. There were thousands of us surrounding this one mound. Drums started beating in the far distance, (If I am ever in a band I'm going to be a drummer.) as they drew closer the crowd parted to let the procession pass through. Eight drummers led a hundred mourners. The sound was as if every heart in the Gathering could be heard beating as one.

"The gathering of our dead," Anree whispered as if I didn't know.

After the drummers came a woman in an antelope headdress. The skin of the antelope flowed down and blended into her hair. On one cheek was painted an eye and on the other a hand. The same symbols are on the locked gates. To my shock and amazement the woman was Shara. The mourners carried clay jars with the ashes of their family members who died during the past year.

The drummers led Shara and the mourners up onto the mound. They processed around the outer bounds of the top of the mound. The drums stopped and Shara spoke to the mourners, but we couldn't hear what she said. The drums played through several rhythms and then silence. The mourners broke their jars and poured the ashes on the mound. After a few minutes of silence the drums started again. One drummer started pounding an even beat and led them all off the mound.

We each had a basket of dirt and climbed up the sides of the mound from every direction. As I struggle up the steep side of the mound, my load was so heavy, I asked Anree if he put rocks in my basket.

Once on top we added our dirt to the mound raising it several feet. Anree and I each brought up two loads of dirt, others made many more trips. When we got up the mound the second time, Anree had tears on his face, at first I thought they were sweat. I asked. "Is it about your parents?"

He wiped the tears, smearing dirt across his cheek. "They were never mourned, as they ought to be mourned, nor remembered, as they ought to be remembered. We never brought them here." I began to cry also.

We spent the rest of the day in games and dances and other festivities.

When Anree and I were alone I told him, "The unicorn was at my house last night."

Without even blinking an eye or cracking a smile he said, "I told you I spoke unicorn."

"You do not speak unicorn."

"So what happened?" Anree asks.

"Larry saw him at his window, came to wake me, but I wasn't there because I was here. By the time he finished searching the house for me the unicorn was gone."

"So, what now?" Anree asks.

I had been thinking about it, so I had a plan. "Tell me what you think of this. I'm going to put the key on a long string and I'm going to ask Larry to put it around the neck of the unicorn if he

144

shows up again." I pause for a minute. "So what do you think?"

"Well it would mean Larry would be helping us and that's good, but will the unicorn bring us the key," he said.

"Well he knew where to find Larry. He can find us if he's meant to." I added smugly. "Or you could ask him to bring us the key."

Anree, ignored my little dig about unicorn speak, "Let's do it."

The key would complete our plan. It would also mean an end to our time together. I'm going to miss Anree. I'm going to miss him a lot. The four conspirators were still talking to people. I didn't think they were having much luck, but if the key and the horn did not deliver a real Tara, they might win and then be out to get rid of us. I might still be needed.

Chapter 22 Thursday Morning
Larry I need Your Help

I breezed through the geometry test. After geometry I ran into Coach in the hall. I'm not sure what possessed me, but I said, "Hey Coach can I meet you in the gym, maybe five minutes after lunch starts?" He agreed and I ran off before he had a chance to ask why.

After fourth period I ran to the locker room, put on my gym clothes and ran out to the gym. My heart was pounding in my chest and a Fire burned in my belly like it never burned in gym class before.

Coach was waiting for me. Seeing me in my gym clothes confused him. With a sarcastic tone he said, "I didn't know you liked gym so much."

I answered with a look that tried to say I don't like gym and this is serious business.

"Okay, so what's this about," he asked.

"I need to do the rope, today, now."

"You won. You and Fred don't have to climb the rope. And in life it doesn't matter whether you climb the rope or not."

"That's true, but it does matter whether or not I ever tried to climb the rope," I said.

"And why can't this wait until tomorrow in gym class," he asked.

"I don't know anything about tomorrow, I only know about today. I need to try today, now," I said with a strain in my voice that even surprised me. I went over and jumped up on the rope.

Wrapping my legs around the rope beneath me, and reaching up a few inches at a time with my right hand and then my left, I moved very slowly up the rope. The Fire in my belly would not let me give up. I worked so hard, the muscles in my arms hurt. I sweated so hard, I thought I would lose my grip, but I kept going. Three feet from the top I stopped. I needed to find something to drive me those final few reaches. I asked myself? If my Dad was watching or Larry or Anree or Tanya would that drive me up these last few feet? No, they wouldn't really matter. That's what I knew now. I had to do this for me. I had to reach deep into Henry to find the strength to let go of the rope and reach up four more times. The whole climb took twenty minutes. The last three feet took ten of those minutes, but I touched my hand to the place where the rope fastened to the steel beam at the top of the gym. I slowly let myself down.

"Wow Henry you did it. I am sorry to say I never thought you would. I'm sorry I under-estimated you."

"Thanks Coach."

I started to go change, but I turned back. "Can I ask you something personal Coach?"

"Probably not, but go ahead and ask."

"Fred says you and Mrs. Ridley get into the same car after school, and you dance pretty well together." Why am I crawling out on this limb? This was none of our business.

"And?" Coach said as a question.

"Well is something up?" I asked.

"In a way," he said laughing. "Mrs. Ridley and I were married last summer."

"Different last names, right?"

"Right," he said.

I ran off to the locker room to change. I climbed the rope, at least one of the week's trials ended well.

Before bed, I went into Larry's room. I had the key on a large loop of heavy string.

"Larry I need you to do something for me tonight. Will you do it?" I asked.

"Depends," he said sounding more like brat Larry than as great little brother Larry.

"The horse will come back tonight," I said.

"He will!" Larry screamed all excited.

"Quiet! Yes, he will. When he wakes you up I want you to come in my room and get me. If I'm not here, I want you to take this key on this string, go out the front door and put it over his head on his neck."

"Where will you be," he said getting all panicked.

"Where I'll be isn't important, but I'll need this key so I can get back." I added that because I thought it would motivate him to help me. "Can you do this for me?"

"I'll do it."

"When I get back I'll tell you all about what has been happening, but until then you still need to keep it a secret. Okay."

"I swear I won't tell," Larry said and I knew he wouldn't. Anree was right. I was lucky to have a little brother. We went to sleep.

Chapter 23 It's Over

Everything ended almost a week ago. They took the journal. I doubt I'll get it back. At first I figured I would quit writing, but I need to write about the final day in Altara in order to get it out of my head. I didn't start writing right away because I didn't want them to see me writing. Somehow they think writing made it happen.

Sometimes I find Mother watching me. She still has a lot of questions, but I think she is afraid of the answers. I promised to never go out at night again, but they didn't believe me. They ordered an alarm system for the house. One day while I was at school they had one of those spy programs loaded on my computer so they could watch everything I do. They gave me a cell phone and said I had to always have it with me and turned on and I better not go over my minutes. The GPS on the phone lets them track me.

I remember those years Anree spent without parents and I know it is better to have parents. The other thing that is nice is I'm hanging with Larry more and Dad is going to take the two of us to the new 3-D movie next week for a boy's night out.

I'm also a better friend now. I've worked to make Tervel and Dante a part of our group. I told Jamal his horn solo in the band was great and I congratulated Fred on a great chess win the other day. The reason I didn't have more friends was because I was a lousy friend. Now that I've gotten that out, I'm ready to tell about my last day in Altara.

Chapter 24
The Last Day in Altara

I woke up alone in our house on top of the mound. We had not been apart since we met. (At least not in Altara.) I thought everything had ended. A Henry must be home in Henry's bed and I must be the Anree in Altara to become the Tara at the ceremony. I thought there would be a good bye, a last word, but we also knew we would rise to what events demanded of us.

A voice called from outside the house, "Hey, you awake yet."

I ran out, I was so glad to see him. Two other guys followed him, but I hardly noticed, I ran up and hugged him.

"I thought you left without saying goodbye," I said.

"I wouldn't do that. And anyway I don't think it's going to happen that way," he said. "I mean, whatever happens, will happen in front of everyone. Remember no more hiding."

"You're right." I now noticed Candor over his shoulder. I turned to see who else he had brought. I couldn't believe it. Standing on top of the tallest mound in Altara was Larry.

"What are you doing here? How did you get here? Let me look at you." I hugged him. He pushed me away.

"Who are you?" Larry said glancing from one Henry to the other. Obviously no one told him who they were going to meet on top of the mound.

"Come tell me, how did you get here?" I said again.

Larry started a little nervously, "Well like I told you earlier," he said pointing to the first Henry he met. "The horse came to my window like before. I went to your room, but you were gone. So I took the key and went out the front door. The horse would let me pet him and stand beside him, but he wouldn't let me put the cord over his head. I kept trying for about twenty minutes. Finally when the horse stood beside the porch I figured he wanted me to climb on his back. So I did. He started running and I closed my eyes and held on. Once when I opened them, it was so dark I couldn't see anything so I kept them closed. I finally opened them as we galloped across open fields. We came up by the gates here, the horse circled around a couple of times and I slipped off. When I stood up, the horse was gone. Some people came up to me and I asked if they knew Henry, but they didn't. So I sat down by the gates and waited."

"Early this morning Candor came to say a confused boy was by the gates asking for someone named Henry. So I went down to the gates and found our little brother. On the way back I picked up some breakfast. Oh and he brought the key."

So we sat down and had breakfast. Larry walked all over the top of the mound looking at the people below. I think he was in shock. Candor sat with us as we talked through the day's plan. Candor would clearly be the Tara's trusted friend and counselor. After breakfast we put the key in one shoulder bag and the horn in the other. We headed down our mound.

151

Rosboes, Hara, Bar and Papo were waiting for us at the bottom. They fell in behind Candor and Larry. We wanted to keep them close so we would know what they were up to and they wanted to be close to us to take advantage of any mistake we made.

As we walked along Candor did his best to answer Larry's questions. Their best conversation was this one.

"I don't know anything about your Anree, but I see two Henrys walking in front of us. Henry has been my brother for as long as I've been alive and I see two Henrys," Larry said.

"Okay, but I see two Anrees and I've known Anree almost my whole life. So one must be Henry and one must be Anree, but which is which," Candor said.

"I'm next to certain the one on the left is Henry," Larry said.

"No that's the one I think is Anree," Candor said.

I finally turned around and said "Look there are two Henrys and two Anrees. That is just how it is."

As soon as I turned back around Candor said to Larry, "I don't think they know which is which anymore." They both laughed, but we didn't. There was truth in Candor's little joke, but today things seemed much clearer. In my mind they were clearer than they had been in days.

We gathered outside the grounds near the fishponds. Again the drummers led the procession, followed by the first troop of dancers, wearing feathered capes. They represented the wind. Rosboes, Bar, Hara and Papo followed, each wore the colors of their village. The four henchmen we had seen them with in the market walked with them. Clearly if there was a confrontation it would be decided by the affections of the people. The second group of dancers wore animal skins, representing the land. We wore blue embroidered capes, we were the river Al. Memere made Anree's cape a long time ago, after we showed ourselves to her and Mora, they and a few other members of the household worked night and day to embroider a second cape. Candor and Larry wore plain red capes and walked at the front of the dancers who represented fire.

As we waited for the processions to begin, Shara came up to us. She dressed as she had for the ritual of the dead. The other guides were with her. She took our right hands and pressing them together touched them to the eye painted on her face saying, "May you always see with understanding." She touched our hands to the painted hand saying, "May your hand always deliver justice." Then the drums started. The guides took their place in the procession with the people of the land. We would never know what they had done to bring together the two Henrys and the two Anrees. I can't even imagine how they managed to bring the unicorn to us. The procession began to move. We carried a heaviness in our hearts. We had no idea how the day would end, but clearly our time together was ending.

The procession divided at the gates, going around them as it had for the past one hundred years. We asked Rosboes, Papo, Hara and Bar to wait for us on the outside of the gates. They waited patiently for us accompanied by their henchmen. I can't imagine what they expected, but when I reached into the Tara's bag and pulled out the key their eyes became as wide as saucers.

I put the key into the lock and the Tara turned it. (That morning when Larry had brought the key, we sent Candor with some graphite to make sure the lock would work.)

Papo with both amazement and respect said, "You are the Tara."

We turned to him and together said, "Yes, we are the Tara." I was still the Tara, but I could feel Henry growing stronger within me. The henchmen faded into the crowd, separating themselves from the losing team. They would not trouble us further.

We opened the gates and walked through to the stomping and cheers of the whole Gathering. Driven by the drums, a mass dance broke out across the grounds. What followed I can only describe as a frenzy. They carried the Tara and I through the crowd on their shoulders at times body surfing us above the crowd. People reached up to touch us. We reached down to touch them. The heaviness left us as we rode on the joy of the crowd. The frenzy did not end until midday when everyone sat down for a banquet. The Tara and I wandered in among the groupings of people, talking and showing the key. Everyone wanted to see the key. The older people said, "Yes, that's the key. It's as my mother (or my father) described it. Yes, yes that's the key. You are the Tara."

At midafternoon we headed back up our mound exhausted. Some of the amazement had worn off for Larry and some practical concerns came to his mind.

"How am I going to get home?" He wanted to know.

"I'm not sure, but you will probably just wake up in your own bed."

"Which one of you is going home with me? One of you is going home with me aren't you?" He desperately wanted some reassurance.

"Your brother will go home with you and the Tara will stay here."

Candor, had taken in everything, and wasn't helping, "Earlier I was joking, but it's true, you don't know do you. You aren't sure who is who and aren't sure what's going to happen."

Larry quietly sobbed. We sat silent for a while.

"You're right Candor. And yes it's scary. But you know what? At the big moments of our lives, we can't ever be absolutely certain what will happen, but here and now, things are starting to become clear. We have always been certain there would be a true Tara, and there is. He opened the gates of Altara and the people proclaimed him the Tara. Before the day is over there will clearly be a Henry. And I have every reason to expect Henry and his brother Larry will return safely to their home. But if you are asking if I know how that will happen, I can only tell you I am excited to wait and see." I didn't say but I also knew Henry would take home the Fire of life he found here. And I knew Henry had learned his anger is a choice, a bad choice about how to face the world. And that his

155

problem with friends was that he wasn't a very good one. And the person responsible for Henry's life is Henry.

The final assembly began an hour before sunset. This marked the end of the Gathering. In the morning most people would return home. Only those who wanted a hearing with the Tara would stay.

We sat on the edge of a low mound. The height gave us a stage where we could be seen and from which we could see all the people of the Gathering seated before us. For the first part of the ceremony people brought us gifts and pledges of gifts. A pledge would be to send a basket of grain or fruit at the time of harvest. These were not taxes or tributes because the Tara neither asked for nor demanded them. These were gifts of heartfelt gratitude. Thanks that the Tara is the Tara.

Often the giver said, "I'm sorry I did not bring two." And we said, "One is too generous of a gift," and we meant it. Besides the gifts of food, there was a beautiful ax carved of jade and similar knives. There were baskets of cloth. There were several knives made from antlers. There were pins and other jewelry made of copper and bronze. We gratefully received and praised all the gifts.

After the giving of gifts the council of four came forward. Each in their turn with a loud voice pledged themselves and their village to the Tara.

"I and the people of Para pledge you our support," said Papo.

"I and the people of Nork pledge you our support," said Hara.

156

"I and the people of Tran pledge you our support," said Bar.

"I and the people of Roan and Rahtol pledge you our support," said Rosboes.

We had brought medallions from the house in Roan and we hung a medallion around each of their necks. Each of the medallions bore the eye and the hand. The gifts surprised them, but not as much as what we said next.

"We are thankful to all the people of the land. We pledge to serve you with the eye of understanding and the hand of justice, but we face a great job and we need the help of many."

"We want these, my Father's good friends, to hear the pleas of justice in their own villages, Alrinar in Para, Hara in Nork, Bar in Tran and Rosboes in Rahtol. Candor and the Tara will hear pleas in Roan."

"For the privilege of serving you," Rosboes began to smile expecting a reward, "these servants of the people will accept no payment and receive no gifts. When all is said and done they are to be no richer and no poorer than they are now."

"And in all disputes, the Tara will hold the final word." The crowd came to their feet stomping and shouting. It was well past sunset and large fires burned on the mound behind us and on the other mounds. When the crowd settled down we turned to the final issue, the unicorn horn.

The people were again seated, but we stood. We began, "Altara bears a wound, a scar, as great as the river Al itself. Many years ago our ancestors took by force what they had no right to take.

Some might say 'not my family', but this horrific act has touched the lives of all of us. Our ancestors caught a unicorn and after wrestling the animal to the ground, they cut the horn from its forehead. This is not a fable or a children's story. This is our story." And we drew the unicorn horn from the bag and held it aloft. The crowd was shocked. "We cannot put back what was taken. We cannot undo what was done. For this wrong we weep in sorrow. Our only hope to set this right is to own the truth and pledge to do right. As your Tara I pledge to see with understanding and to act with justice."

The people came to their feet stomping and shouting, after ten minutes though they grew silent. They pointed up behind us. The hornless unicorn stood silhouetted by the fires behind us.

We went up to him. We each put a hand on the scar. The pain was less. The Tara held aloft the horn. I thought lightening would strike as it had the night of the Taking. Instead a silence, like the still silence of a heavy snow fall, covered the Gathering.

After a few minutes a powerful wind roared over the Gathering breaking the silence and carrying embers and flames of the fires high into the air above us. The horn turned to dust in his hand. The wind carried the dust away. None touched the ground. We no longer bore the burden of our parent's wrongs. The land no longer bore the scar. He stood before all as the first true Tara in a hundred years.

The unicorn began to circle around the top of the mound, at first, as though running for enjoyment, but then with a purpose.

I was Henry and only Henry. I no longer belonged here in this time or place. There would be no more surprises. The people might not know how there came to be two Taras, but they would remember how the two Taras became the one true Tara. I hugged the Tara and Candor. Larry, the Tara and Candor hugged. Our hearts filled with sadness and joy.

I leapt on to the back of the unicorn. I pulled Larry up behind me. We circled once around the top of the mound and then down through the people. The crowd parted for us, creating an avenue leading through the gates, past the ponds and out of Altara. We headed west up the Northern Road, across the hunting grounds up into the mountains and through Lothar. Whether this was Lothar of the past or Lothar of the future I don't know. In place of the ruin, we passed through the grounds of a majestic lodge grander than I had imagined.

As we enter the darkness Larry asked, "Are you Henry?"

I answered, "I am your brother."

Chapter 25 Friday Morning
Alive In Suborediom

Larry and I woke up in our beds on Friday morning. I didn't know how or why. I remembered riding through Lothar and into the darkness and then I raised my head up off my pillow to see my Mother sitting at my desk reading my journal. The sight sent a shiver running through my body. I dropped my head down into my pillow face first.

"What is this?" she shouted pointing to the journal. "Where have you been? Where is your brother? How did you get back here? The police are looking for you." Adults do that, they ask a lot of questions and don't even pause for you to answer. I think they do it because your answers won't make anything better.

She picked up her phone, called my Father and walked out of my room. I guessed to go check on Larry. My Father, the police and the whole world were searching for us. As I understand things, Mother woke up at two and decided to check on us. When she found us missing, she woke my Father. After they searched the house they called the police. The police had them call Fred and Jamal's parents to see if we were there or if they were missing. Then, even though Fred told them we had broken up, they called Tanya's house.

While they looked for us, Mother sat down in my room, discovered the journal, and started reading.

My Father came home followed by the police ten minutes later. They went away after talking to my parents.

The three of us sat down in the den. No one yelled, or screamed. Everyone was very calm and very tense, very tense. The conversation began by Mother giving a short synopsis of what she read in the journal.

My Father looked at me with a restrained anger, "You mean every night for the past two weeks, instead of going to bed you've been running off to some virtual reality."

"All I know is that I fall asleep in my bed and I wake up in Altara, and if I fall asleep in Altara I wake up here in my bed. After the first night I started writing it all down. So I've been writing about everything."

"And last night what happened last night," Mother demanded.

"Last night Larry brought me the key."

"The one Granddad gave you?" she asked.

"Yes, and the Tara became the true Tara, and Larry and I came home." I consciously gave them the short version of the story.

After that they sent me to my room. It was time to get ready for school so I started getting dressed. When Larry woke up I told him they knew we were gone last night and he should lay low. Instead, he bounded into the den telling every detail of his experience in Altara. When I came into the den ready to leave for school he was talking about the first time he saw the second Henry. To my thankful surprise they let me go to school. As I walked to the bus stop, I realized they sent me to school in order to give themselves time to calm down and decide what to do.

On the bus Fred tells everyone the police called his house at three a.m. looking for me. Then he launched into twenty questions, just like an adult.

"Did you ride in a police car?"

"Are you going to jail?"

"Are you going to reform school?"

"Are you grounded for life?"

"Where did you go?"

"Why did you take Larry?"

When he finally stopped, I told him this was all a big misunderstanding.

In gym class I climbed the rope in front of the whole class. At the end of class Coach called me over and said, "I understand something happened last night, if you want to talk come see me." That felt good and I said, maybe next week I would, but I haven't yet.

At lunch Tanya came to sit with me and said I should call her. She thought I was more interesting because the police called in the middle of the night hunting for me. I am more interesting because I know more about what it means to be Henry. I said we could be friends, and that I had recently learned how important friends are.

In fifth period a note came from the office saying I was dismissed early for a doctor's appointment. This was the first I heard about a doctor's appointment. My Mother waited at the front of the school. We rode in silence. I had no idea why I was being taken to the doctor. I wondered if doctors fitted you for those ankle

162

bracelets that monitor your whereabouts, or maybe the doctor would insert a GPS chip beneath my skin so they could track me.

To my surprise we pulled up at my pediatricians' office. I hadn't been there in two years. He gave me a basic physical, like I had before going to camp last summer, then he sent me out while he talked to my Mother. She came out of the back and headed straight out the front door. I dropped the Highlights magazine I was looking at and scrambled after her.

We now went to the doctor that gave me my camp physical and repeated the same process. I was still at a loss to understand what was going on. We left there just as abruptly.

When we pulled up to my dentist's office I realized the issue was not my health. The issue was my identity. After the dentist said several times the insurance wasn't going to pay for these, they took a full set of front and side x-rays. Then my Mother and the dentist stood comparing them to the x-rays from six months ago. I never had any cavities or fillings. They only had teeth to compare to teeth. Finally the dentist said, "Of course his jaw has grown a little, but these look like the same teeth to me. And he looks like Henry to me. Do you really think he might not be your son?"

"I'm sorry. It's just a Mom thing," she said grabbing me and going.

As we waited for the elevator outside the dentist's office I said, "It's about whether or not I'm Henry?"

"Yes, Larry told us about what Candor said about the two of you and he told us that when he

163

asked if you were Henry you didn't really answer him."

I very quietly said, "I am Henry. I am more Henry than I've ever been."

She just as quietly, but very sternly said, "Are you my Henry?"

"Even if I am the Henry, who was Anree, don't I need a family and a Mother and someone to love me?"

There was silence, a pause as long as the river Al.

She stretched her arms around me and drew me close. We both cried. I don't ever remember being hugged with so much love and I didn't push her away.

I am Henry on Fire and alive in Suborediom.

(Thanks for reading. Thinking that someone might care enough about my life to ever read this, kept me writing.)

Henry

Henry's Rules

Henry Rule Number One: Don't watch other guys while they take whizzes.

Henry Rule Number Two: Smelly boys are not lucky boys.

Henry Rule Number Three: If you don't know where you are going why does it matter which road you take.

Henry Rule Number Four: It is always good to know what your opponent is thinking.

Henry Rule Number Five: Note to self, Shut up.

Henry Rule Number Six: People only have the power over you that you give them.

Henry Rule Number Seven: Just because you might fail at something, is not a reason not to try

Henry Rule Number Eight: Usually the stuff you don't want to do is more important than the stuff you want to do.

Dad's Man Rules

Man Rule Number One: No matter how many times I drive past that gas station, I will not stop and ask directions.

Man Rule Number Two: Even if the earth opens and swallows me alive, I will not change my plans.

Man Rule Number Three: Boys fight, men talk.

Man Rule Number Four: (This rule never came up.)

Man Rule Number Five: You always have choices.
You may not like your choices but you
have choices.

The Tara's Wisdom
Always be honest with people.
The less you say, the more they will tell.
People have no power over you, except the power
you give them.
The power of the Tara comes from the love of the
people.
The river flows always to the sea, but not so the
wind or the affections of the heart,

Discussion Questions
1. Which boy do you think returned in the
   end? What convinces you?
2. If they are identical, does it matter which
   boy returned?
3. Which one of Henry's rules do you think is
   the most important?
4. Write five rules of your own.
5. Do you think the thirteen-year-old Tara is
   ready to lead his people? Why?
6. Was this all a dream or did Henry go to a
   real place?
7. Henry says he learned he was a lousy
   friend. What makes someone a good
   friend?

This book is a work of fiction. Names, characters, places and incidents are either a work of the authors imagination or are used fictitiously and any resemblance to actual persons living or dead business establishments, events or locales is accidental. Except for the following footnoted exceptions.

Chapter 2 To my knowledge Henry's Dad never met any of the people who founded Wikipedia.

Chapter 5 The chess match is based on Cathy Forbes playing Bobby Fischer 1992, which at the time of this writing could be found at: http://www.chessgames.com/

Chapter 9 Alice meets the Cheshire Cat in Chapter 6 of Alice in Wonderland by Lewis Carroll.

Chapter 15 The scene from Treasure Island by Robert Louis Stevenson is found in Chapter seven.

Chapter 19 The image of the mound city, Altara, and of the Eye and Hand are drawn from Moundville Archeological Park in Alabama, a large settlement of Mississippian culture on the Black Warrior River in central Alabama. (I added the gates.) I found this to be a place of great inspiration.

Acknowledgements

I would like to thank the many people who read various versions of this manuscript and who offered me support. I thank Debbie Madden, who transformed my handwritten second draft into typed text. I appreciate the workshops and conferences of SCBWI. I thank my brother Mike and MaryAnn Diorio who line edited earlier versions. (They are not responsible for any errors in this final publication.) I thank Rich Wallace for his writer's workshop at the Highlight Foundation. I thank Chris Greene, who provided me with the formula for the volume of a truncated square pyramid. I am thankful to author Leslie Meier who has always been an inspiration to me. And I am most grateful for my wife Pam who loves me.

About the Author

Stuart grew up in the suburbs of Houston. He wrote the first draft of Henry on Fire while on vacation at the beach, writing one day and night of the story each day.

Stuart lives and writes at his home, Greenway Cottage, on the edge of the Virginia Piedmont. You can keep up with Stuart through his blog site, www.by-stuart.com.

Book two: <u>Henry and the ShadowMan Band</u>

Henry's story continues with problems in Altara and at home in suburban Fairdale.

In Altara Henry and Anree fight off wild dogs and mountain lions, battle the sea in a hurricane; find the bones of Anree's parents and confront the man who murdered them.

At home Henry, Jamal and Fred start a band only to be joined by a new kid on the block who doesn't speak and who can see into the world of Altara. And Henry's problems with girls continue when his mother tells three girls that the boys would love to have them join the band.

Book three: <u>Henry in Stand with Fred Friday</u>

Anree arrives unannounced and unexpected at Henry's school in suburbia because Henry needs his help. Unfortunately Anree can't keep from causing problems for Henry, beginning with a school detention he gets within minutes of arriving, but maybe he makes up for that by getting Henry a date with Jania for the school dance on Friday.

Anree hides in the boy's restroom during the next to the last class period and over hears a plot to prank Henry's friend Fred, but doesn't know how to stop it. Fred is pranked and walks home from school in a dress. However Fred refuses to name

169

the bullies who pranked him and the boys have to
decide how to achieve justice for Fred. Anree
thinks the answer is for all the guys to wear dresses
to school on Friday. Henry repeatedly says no.

On the first day Henry wonders if he will survive
Anree's help, but in the end he won't survive a life
threatening accident without him.